A Shade Of

Vampire

Book 1

Bella Forrest

Contents

PROLOGUE

I never once imagined that my life would play out the way it did. To be fair, I guess one could say that life never really unfolds the way we expect it to.

I know my father's didn't, but I doubt there's a teenager in the world who could have expected her life to play out like mine.

I'd just turned seventeen when my life changed completely and irreversibly. It was only one night before that I was thinking of the future, of my dreams and aspirations. I wanted to become a social worker or even a lawyer in hopes of helping others like me who were abandoned by their families. It was my birthday, and at my age, it felt like I had my whole life ahead of me. Granted, I didn't believe it would be a great life, but at least I was certain I was going to have *a life*.

That following evening, I wasn't so sure any more. How could I have been when, within the span of twenty four hours, I'd gone from high school senior and certified wallflower to captive of the prince of the largest and most powerful coven of our time?

When I was nine years old, my mother, Camilla, was sent to a lunatic asylum. I'd always known that there was something strange about my mother, but I never expected her to completely lose her mind. What happened to her left its mark on me.

After this, my main goal in life was to survive without losing my mind and turning out like my mother.

Then, after *it* happened, on the evening of my seventeenth birthday, my only goal was *to survive*. Never mind my fear of going insane. I was convinced that I'd already gone crazy anyway.

There was no way to predict what would happen to me after that night.

During her better days, my mother had given me a warning. She said that I should expect life to dish out my own fair share of surprises.

But Derek Novak was a surprise that was far from fair…

Chapter 1: Sofia

I was taking an evening stroll along the beach, feeling the smooth sand under my bare feet with every step. The rhythmic crashing of heavy waves against the shore soothed my ears. My skin was tingling with every blow of the gentle summer breeze, the distinct scent of ocean salt filling my nostrils. As I dabbed cherry-flavored Chapstick over my parched lips, they formed a bitter smile. The balm only served to add its sweet taste to the numerous sensations engulfing me at that particular moment.

I've always found myself completely attuned to all five of my senses, but that night, I was to all but one. My sight was blurred by the tears I was fighting to hold back. I couldn't appreciate the exotic scene around me. All I could think about was the disappointed expression on my best friend's handsome face.

Benjamin Hudson was the only person in the world who could make me feel the way I did that night.

Perhaps the sorrow I felt was mostly due to the fact that I still held expectations – expectations I knew would only ever cause me pain.

I reasoned to myself that I had the right to be hurt. It was my birthday. He was my best friend. He shouldn't have forgotten.

But he did. Again.

I knew the disappointment in his chiseled face was more toward himself than me. I knew he could beat himself up endlessly over his careless slip-ups, and do believe me when I say that he had many of those. So, that night, I was wondering to myself whether I had just over-reacted.

I would find myself deciding that I did, in fact, over-react and that it was time to stop wallowing. I'd turn back toward the villa the Hudsons rented for their family vacation, determined to just start having fun again with the most important person in my life, but then I'd remember…

I'd remember what it felt like to see him with his arms around Tanya Wilson, the gorgeous blonde he'd had the hots for all summer.

The image quickly threw all thoughts of kissing and making up with Ben out the window.

"Gosh, Sofia… I'm so sorry… I'm an awful best friend…" were the words that came out of his mouth when he realized his mistake. I walked out on him and ended up at the beach, wanting to hit myself over the head for being so sensitive.

I was being unfair. After all, it wasn't Ben's fault that I fell for the biggest cliché of all time when I decided to grow non-best-friend-like feelings for my best friend. That was why seeing him with Tanya hurt so much, especially realizing that I could never be like Tanya. I simply wasn't the type of girl a guy like Ben would go for. I knew that and yet I still allowed myself to fall for his charms. I hated myself for it, but it was what it was. At that time, I was so sure that he was indeed the "love of my life".

But could anyone really blame me for how I felt around him?

Ben was as dreamy as dreamy gets. He was tall, well-built, smart and had that dashing smile that would put to shame those of the models gracing the covers of any magazine. He was fun, confident and popular. He was also sweet and kind whenever he wanted to be. More than any of that, he *saw* me. He gave me the time of day when no one else – not even my own parents – would. It was with Ben that I never felt invisible…except when Tanya was around.

As I took that evening walk, I knew I was fooling myself. There was no way I could stay mad at Ben for long. I liked to think of myself as strong and independent, but truth be told, I couldn't imagine a life without Ben in it. My dependence on him scared me. It was frightening realizing that I needed another person as much as I needed him.

I'd been meandering along the shore for about an hour when I suddenly sensed that I wasn't alone. Someone was approaching me from behind. My heart leaped. I was so sure it was Ben, that when a stranger showed up beside me, I couldn't hide my disappointment.

He must have noticed, because a smirk formed on his lips. "Were you expecting someone else, love?"

I eyed him suspiciously, looking him over and taking in his appearance. My eyes widened. I couldn't find words to describe how fine a man he was. He was almost beautiful. The first thing I took notice of was how his blue eyes were about three shades brighter than any I'd ever seen before. It was such a stark contrast to his pale – almost white – skin and dark hair. Standing beside me, he was easily more than half a foot taller. His height, broad shoulders and lean build reminded me of Ben, but he had a presence that was far more imposing than my best friend's.

My gaze settled on his face.

I realized that he was inspecting me just as closely as I was him. His gaze suddenly made me feel uncomfortably vulnerable. I gave my father's advice to never speak to strangers a second thought, but quickly canceled out all notions of heeding to his counsel when I reminded myself that he stopped caring long ago.

I straightened to my full height and mustered all the courage I had to keep myself from running away from this stranger.

Big mistake.

The confident smirk didn't leave his face for even a moment.

"Like what you see?"

"A bit full of yourself, aren't you?" I said, annoyed by his audacity.

He stepped forward and leaned his head toward mine.

"Don't I have the right to be?"

He knew he looked good and wasn't about to act like he didn't.

"Whatever," was my oh-so-brilliant comeback.

Unsettled by how close he was now, I rolled my eyes and did a one-eighty, not quite in the mood to play whatever game this stranger was proposing.

I would soon realize that I was about to play his game whether I liked it or not.

He grabbed my arm and turned my body to face him. His motion made every single internal alarm I had within me, go off in a frenzy.

This man was danger and I knew it. I tried to wriggle away from his touch, but I was no match for his strength.

"Tell me your name," he commanded.

I was about to refuse, but was horrified to find myself blurting out my name in response.

"Sofia Claremont."

As soon as I revealed my name, his eyes lit up with a kind of sinister approval. Then he reached for my face and traced his thumb over my jaw line.

"Hello, Sofia Claremont. You're one stupid girl for taking a walk alone at this time of night. You never know what kind of evil a pretty little thing like you could happen to come by."

I found myself wondering exactly what kind of evil he was. But I was suddenly overcome by the sensations that were surrounding me. My senses took in everything at once. I heard the waves, felt the sand, smelled the ocean salt, tasted the flavor of cherry and saw the stranger's manic appearance as he stuck a needle to my neck. The effect was instant. I was barely able to gasp, much less scream. I went from sensing *everything* to sensing absolutely nothing.

My last conscious thought was that I may never see Ben again.

Chapter 2: Sofia

I blinked several times, hoping that I would see more clearly if I did it enough. No chance. I was enveloped by darkness and it didn't look like that was about to change any time soon.

I sensed my claustrophobia about to kick in, afraid that, for all I knew, I could be in some sort of extremely enclosed space, but the cold, airy feel of the room soon assured me that I was not.

I tried to move about the space and quickly realized that the lack of lighting was the least of my concerns. For one thing, I was being held by metal restraints on my wrists and ankles.

I could barely raise my arms without a considerable amount of effort. I tried to pull against my chains. They were fastened to the wall.

I ran my hands over my body and felt the soft linen fabric of the white cover-up I had pulled over my swimsuit before my untimely walk earlier that evening. I had intended to go for a swim.

Yet another one of your brilliant ideas, Sofia. Now you're locked up in a dungeon wearing your swimsuit and a cover-up that's nowhere near warm enough to fend off the biting cold.

I gritted my teeth, loathing myself for being so careless about my own safety. I caught myself before I could turn myself into my own personal villain. The severity of the situation hit me full force and I was unable to suppress a shudder.

What have I gotten myself into?

Despite the cold, I suddenly felt sweat forming on my forehead.

I'm in a dungeon.

The word alone caused alternating images of stories I'd read about places like the London Tower and the kinds of torture prisoners endured there. I balled my fists, realizing for the first time how much I loved my fingers, as images flit through my mind of someone sticking sharp objects underneath my nails.

If my goal in life was to not go insane, this sure was not helping me meet my objective.

I sank to the ground, pulling my legs against my chest with my arms, remembering all those times I felt like something was wrong with me. Familiar fears of turning out like my mother began to assault me. Growing up, I'd seen psychologist after psychologist trying to figure out "what was wrong with me". I apparently had ADHD when I was a kid, OCD during my preteen years. Just recently, they were testing me for bipolar disorder. Given this situation, I was sure I'd develop an extra disorder or two.

Let's add post-traumatic-stress disorder to the bunch.

Then I heard sounds – echoing footsteps – coming from outside the room I was in.

Eight seconds later, the door unlocked and swung open. The incandescent lighting flickered on. It took a couple of seconds for my eyes to adjust to the sudden flow of light. My first instinct was to take in every detail of the room I was in. It looked less archaic than it was in my imagination. The walls were actually made of concrete, not stone like the castles of old.

I stared at the floor and frowned in confusion at the straw beneath my feet.

"The hay adds a nice touch, I think. Makes our captives feel like they somehow time traveled to the Dark Ages."

My eyes were quickly drawn to the source of the voice. All I could do was glare at him.

It was the stranger from the beach.

There were so many questions I wanted him to answer, so many curses I wanted to blurt out, but I held my tongue. Considering my predicament and my very limited mobility, irking my captor didn't seem like the wisest thing to do.

He eyed me from head to foot the same way he did when we were back at the beach. This time, however, I could sense his hunger. He was a predator. I was his prey. I shuddered to think exactly what kind of predator had just caught me in his trap.

His eyes were spanning the length of my legs as he approached me. He seemed to find amusement in my anxiety.

He stopped about a foot away from me and grinned as he studied me closely. The fact that he seemed pleased by what he saw made the situation even scarier.

"Who are you?! What do you want from me?!"

I asked the questions not so I could hear the answers. I just needed to break the silence, in hopes of hiding my erratic heartbeats.

He raised his hand and brushed a stray strand of hair away from my face. I flinched at his touch. He then pushed me against the wall and pinned me to it, leaning his full weight against me. It felt like he was trying to crush my ribs along with every other internal organ.

"Welcome to The Shade, Sofia." He leaned closer, his breath cool against my ear. "You really are quite a beauty, aren't you?"

From his lips, it sounded more like an insult than a compliment.

My fears were being replaced with anger. I gathered all the strength I could to lift my hands in an attempt to push him away. As I struggled, I became fully aware of the coarseness of the concrete wall behind me, scratching through the sheerness of my cover-up and grating against my skin.

He chuckled when I failed to budge him even slightly.

"You'll only hurt yourself."

"I demand that you let go of me. Now." I said the words with more confidence than I felt.

If there was even the slightest trace of true confidence in me, he managed to make it disappear when he grabbed a clump of my hair with one hand and my jaw with the other. He leaned his face even closer to mine, the tips of our noses almost touching.

"It will do you well to learn that here, you are not in a place to make impetuous demands." The words hissed from his lips.

It was appropriate for him; he was revealing to me exactly what he was. A snake. His hands eased out of my hair and away from my jaw before he began to freely grope my body in places no other person other than myself had ever touched before. His eyes never left mine even as I tried to wither away from his touch.

"There's no escape, Sofia. If you want to survive, you must realize that in this kingdom, you exist to obey. Do as you're told and we just might allow you to live."

I spat on his face. It was the only act of defiance I could manage with his weight against me.

My feeling of victory lasted for about a second. He wiped his face clean with the back of his hand and then gripped the nape of my neck.

"You asked me what I wanted from you. There really is only one thing you could give me, Sofia."

I glared at him, determined to die with dignity and self-respect.

"Oh? And what's that?"

His answer sent chills down my spine.

"*You.*"

Before I could even let his statement fully register, sharp fangs protruded from his mouth. He pushed my head to the side, exposing my neck. It felt like I was in a dream but, as much as I tried to pinch myself awake, there was no escaping it.

I was convinced that my greatest fear had come to pass. I'd already gone insane, because at that moment, I was certain that I was about to be eaten alive by a vampire.

Chapter 3: Sofia

"Lucas!"

I could already feel the sharp edge of his fangs piercing my skin when a shrill female voice brought me an unexpected reprieve.

He growled with frustration and roughly pushed me away, causing my head to jerk back and bump against the concrete wall.

I glared every sort of sharp blade imaginable at my captor. *So your name is Lucas.*

He seemed to be reading my mind, because an ugly frown marred his handsome features.

"Yes. The name's Lucas, my sweet innocent. Not that knowing this will do you any good."

"What do you think you're doing?!" The female voice demanded of him.

I strained my neck to see who my savior was, but Lucas was blocking my view.

"What do you *think* I'm doing, Vivienne?"

His chest heaved as he said the words. He looked just about ready to rip the head off of this Vivienne woman.

"So sorry about this, Sofia dear."

Of course. How dare she interrupt your dinner. Happy birthday, Sofia. You just happen to be the birthday feast.

He looked at me as though I was his ally.

"It seems my sister couldn't just let things be."

My heart sank at that piece of information. How could I expect this creature's sister to help me get out of the nightmare he'd brought me into? Her next words cemented my fears and made it clear that there was no escaping my doom. At least, not with her help.

"She isn't yours to feast on."

"*I* found her!" Lucas shouted with indignation.

"You found her *for Derek*."

I was already busy musing over what these words implied. *Save me from one vampire so another can sup on me instead.* I wasn't too preoccupied, however, to ignore the change of expression on Lucas' face at the mention of this Derek person.

"She's just one girl, Vivienne. What harm would it do to take one girl for myself? I always get to keep the lovelies I find on these hunts. *Always*."

"You already have plenty of beautiful women in your quarters. You need not keep this one. Corrine made it clear that the young women found tonight are to be reserved for when Derek wakes up."

Lucas eyed me intently. He was looking at me so closely that I was sure he was already well-acquainted with every single mole and freckle on my face.

I could see his Adam's apple move as he gulped, deprived of the morsel he was so desperate to have. I wasn't sure what to feel. I was relieved to escape Lucas, but now I was filled with dread over who Derek was.

Lucas once again took my face in his hands and traced his thumb over my lips.

"This fragile little twig couldn't possibly be the one. I don't understand why everyone seems to worship the ground Corrine walks on. No matter what that witch says, Sleeping Beauty has shown no signs of waking up any time soon."

"Derek will wake up soon. The sooner you accept that, the better off we'll all be."

"I'm your brother too. Why do you constantly choose him over me?"

"Despite what you think, it has nothing to do with the fact that he's my twin. It has everything to do with who you are and who he is. I love you, brother, but you must accept that you weren't meant to rule."

Her words were spoken firmly, but with an unmistakable hint of affection.

I could see the pain in Lucas' eyes at this bold statement coming from his own sister. At that point, I knew I must have truly gone mad, because I actually felt sorry for him. I knew what he felt, what it was like to have no one on your side. I didn't think anyone deserved to feel that way.

He quickly reminded me, however, that he was my tormentor and made me completely reconsider my stand in the matter. Whatever anger or sadness he felt, he took out on me. He clamped one hand over my neck, constricting my breathing. A claw protruded from the thumb he had over my lips and he began pressing the end of it over my mouth. I whimpered as his sharp nail drew a small line of blood over my sensitive lower lip.

"Lucas! Stop it now!" Vivienne once again raised her voice in reprimand.

He let go of me, allowing me to gasp for breath. He backed away and stared down at me like I was the most disgusting thing he'd ever seen in his life.

"I'm just trying to help you wake your beloved *Derek* up, Vivienne. Take this little minx to him and make her kiss the Sleeping Beauty. The taste of her blood just might wake the Prince up."

He began to head for the door, but stopped to glare at his sister before completely heading off.

"Isn't that how you think all this is going to play out when he wakes up? Just like a fairy tale?"

A wave of relief washed over me when he finally left the room. The words exchanged by the siblings remained in my head, but I was too overcome by emotion to even attempt to make sense of them. My knees were shaking so I gave in and sank to the ground before finally looking up to see what Vivienne looked like.

If I thought Lucas could be beautiful, Vivienne was far more stunning to behold. She was a couple of inches shorter than her brother, but had the same dark hair and pale complexion. Her eyes, however, were different. Against the light in the room, they almost looked violet.

She was eyeing me warily, as if I was a heavy burden she had to bear.

"Thank you," I told her, genuinely meaning it even though I had no idea what she had in store for me.

There was a deadpan expression on her face as she looked at me.

"Understand, girl, that you are nothing here. You're nothing but a pawn, a piece used to make the board move. Your best chance at survival and proving your significance is to win Derek's affections.

Considering everything I know about my brother, I'm not sure that's even possible."

Her words dealt my hope a final crushing blow. She made it perfectly clear that wherever this place called The Shade was, I had no allies. No friends.

I had only myself to rely on. And that, I thought, was the most frightening aspect of my predicament. After all, how could I rely on someone I couldn't trust?

Chapter 4: Derek

The moment my eyes opened, I could hear everything, smell everything and feel everything within at least a quarter-mile radius from me. I was sure that the sensation alone would bring my body into complete shock, until my vision settled on a familiar face. The woman I had trusted enough to provide my escape from everything.

"Cora?"

It was strange. The last thing I remembered was Cora's face as I'd faded off into slumber. It felt like I had only slept for a few moments before being jolted awake. I wondered if something had gone wrong with the spell. Looking at the witch, I wondered how it was possible that she looked younger. I found my answer when the buxom beauty with light brown skin and cascading locks of chestnut hair shook her head.

"I'm not Cora. I'm Corrine."

I lifted myself up from the slab of stone that had served as my resting place … for how long, I could only muse. I took in my surroundings - I was in a candlelit hall with marble floors and giant pillars. The first word that came to mind when I surveyed the place was *sanctuary*.

I eyed the young woman, wary of her intentions. It took a moment for her strange clothes to register. I became aware of how I was dressed and realized that perhaps more time had passed than I had initially thought. But at that point, it didn't really matter.

I wasn't supposed to wake up. *Ever*.

Contemptuous that I should wake when I'd so explicitly asked for an eternal escape, I shouted a command as prince of The Shade.

"I want to see Cora. Bring her to me."

I hated the authoritative tone my voice naturally took on. Who was I to issue commands? I was no prince – much less the savior Vivienne painted me to be.

The prophecy she spoke soon after we were turned into vampires immediately haunted me as I recalled it.

The younger will rule above father and brother and his reign alone can provide his kind true sanctuary.

I still remember the look on Vivienne's face when she uttered those words. More than that, I saw the expressions of my father and brother. Resentment.

I snapped myself out of the bout of nostalgia I was sinking into and raised a brow at the woman before me. *Why isn't she moving?*

Despite my misgivings about ruling, I wasn't used to others not obeying me. After a hundred years of fighting for survival and leading my coven to The Shade, I'd grown accustomed to being revered and followed. I wasn't sure I liked that about myself, but it was what it was.

"Would you like us to dig her grave up, your highness? I doubt her corpse will do much good to clarify whatever questions you have in mind."

I grimaced. *Your highness.* A reminder of the day my father took to heart the coven's silly notion to establish himself as King of The Shade. However, the title did not bother me as much as the news of Cora's demise and this young woman's manner of addressing me. I swallowed hard as I grabbed the edges of the stone slab I was sitting on.

The sensations coursing through my veins made it clear exactly what my body was now screaming out for. Blood. I was famished. Another bitter reminder of the past I meant to escape when I gave the witch permission to put a sleeping curse on me.

Desperate to divert my thoughts to other matters, I shifted my gaze toward Corrine.

"Who are you?"

"I'm the witch of The Shade, descendant of the great witch, Cora."

I paused, keeping my eyes on her. That information alone commanded my respect. *No wonder she speaks to me as she does.* If she was Cora's descendent, it was better to keep her as ally rather than foe. I heaved a sigh, not sure I wanted to hear the answer to my next question.

"What century is it?"

"The twenty-first."

I diverted my gaze away from her as I let that information register. *Four hundred years. I escaped for four hundred years.*

Corrine began circling me like a vulture. I could sense her distrust. She was scrutinizing me, perhaps wondering what my awakening meant for The Shade.

I wanted to tell her that it meant nothing, because I fully intended to escape from it all over again. But there were so many questions running through my mind.

"Why am I awake?"

"It's simply time."

I clenched my fists. "Time for what?"

"For Derek Novak to stop acting like a coward and face what he was meant to do. Rule."

My jaw tightened. "I didn't ask for this."

"Neither did any of us, but if his highness is entertaining any notions of going back to his dreamy reprieve, then I suggest you forget them now, Prince. Until you've played your part, there's no means of escape. Cora made certain of that."

"What do you mean…"

Before I could finish my question, the acacia doors swung open and my older brother and twin sister strode into the chamber.

Lucas gave me a curt nod. I nodded back. That was the closest we ever got to showing each other brotherly affection.

Vivienne, on the other hand, threw her arms around my neck, whispering how glad she was that I was finally awake.

"That makes one of us." I couldn't keep myself from telling her exactly what I felt.

And then it happened. My gut clenched excruciatingly. The smell was overwhelming – almost intoxicating. When I saw them, I cursed the person whose idea it was to bring about this kind of cruelty upon my wake.

As my sister stepped aside to allow me full view, I remembered everything. I remembered why it was so important for me to stay asleep.

Five beautiful young women – innocents – no older than I was when I became a vampire, stood before me. I sensed their fear, but the predator within me was desperate for release. I hated myself for it, but I wanted nothing more than to suck every last drop of blood out of every single one of them.

Chapter 5: Sofia

My eyes were glued to the young man Vivienne embraced. There was no question in my mind that it was him. He was the one Vivienne told Lucas I was here for. He was the one the guards and servants were whispering about. He was Derek Novak.

Soon after Vivienne left me inside the dungeon, guards arrived to escort me, along several other girls around my age, out of the network of underground caves they called The Cells. I assumed they were The Shade's prison system.

Once out in the open, I stumbled forward and found myself surrounded by the tallest trees I'd ever seen – giant redwoods that I'd only ever read about in books. I turned around to look at The Cells' exit. In the moonlight, I could make out a giant oak doorway fixed into a jagged grey-stone wall. My eyes shot upward, trying to gauge the height and structure of the building. That's when I realized that this was no building. We were standing at the foot of a colossal mountain, it's sharp peaks towering over us. The intricate tunnels and chambers that consisted of The Cells were built within the bowels of a sprawling mountain range.

From The Cells, the guards ordered us girls to form a single line and follow them as they guided us onto a well-traveled dirt pathway leading into a dark, murky wood. My teeth chattered as they herded us beneath the shadows of the wiry branches. It wasn't really the cold that was making me shudder, though the howling wind certainly wasn't helping. It was that everything about the forest we'd entered reminded me of those I'd read about in fairy tales – home to big bad wolves and nocturnal creatures waiting to devour any unfortunate passerby. At that point, I regretted ever watching horror movies, because I was certain that we were being led to a painful, grisly death.

At the mercy of vampires. I shut my eyes and tried to shake the thought away.

It had probably been less than twenty minutes, but it felt as though we'd been walking for hours by the time an exit from that haunted wood came into view. We stepped into a large clearing.

"This, lovelies," one of the guards spoke up, without bothering to hide the way he was leering at us, "is The Vale."

The dirt path we were trekking along eventually led to a cobblestone street that was teeming with life. It was clearly some sort of hub for trade, based on the large crowds of people milling about the place - as if it were the most normal thing in the world to go to market at this unholy hour of the night.

I almost forgot my fear for a moment as my eyes widened with fascination. Parts of The Vale looked like a town that had popped right out of the medieval era. The streets were lit with burning lanterns. Thatched roofs, clay exteriors, tents housing a variety of wares. Some buildings, on the other hand, made me tilt my head to the side, wondering what exactly they were for, considering their unique geometric and angular architectural designs. It was almost as if we were in a town that managed to mix the past and the future in one place and I began wondering how long it had been since The Vale first came into existence.

We took half a dozen turns through the maze of streets until we were led to the front door of a two-storey building, whose exteriors were painted with cool pastel colors. It looked out-of-place compared to the dark vibe I was getting from the rest of The Shade.

We were ushered through the double glass doors and I found myself utterly confused. I was expecting to be brought to some sort of dungeon or interrogation room – some place dark and foreboding. Instead, we were brought to … a spa. The smell of jasmine and lavender, the sound of gushing fountains, the cool, rhythmic music … I had no idea what to make of the whole thing.

I soon learned that they called the place "The Baths". Upon entering the building's lobby, the guards immediately handed us over to the care of several young women.

From there, each of us was ushered into a series of beauty regimens; a warm bath, massages, manicures, pedicures and facials. We were perfumed with scents that I found absolutely intoxicating. Finally, we were led into a dressing room where a dark-haired woman handed us parcels that contained what we were to wear. I felt my gut clench when I saw the lacy lingerie and the pearl white gown I had been given.

It dawned on me suddenly what all these beauty treatments were for. They were preparing us for *him*. I found myself shaking as I slipped on the garments, the gown hugging my curves at just the right places. I checked the way I looked in front of a full-length mirror and drew a breath. I couldn't remember ever feeling more beautiful than I did at that moment, and yet, I felt nothing but absolute dread. I knew it was not to a young girl's advantage to look stunning at The Shade.

"You look gorgeous," the dark-haired woman told me, as she helped zip up my dress from the back.

"What's all this for?" I asked in a hoarse whisper.

Watching her in the mirror's reflection, the sadness that traced her pretty round face didn't escape my notice.

"Rumors are that you girls are to be part of the prince's harem. All of The Shade's Elite have harems of their own. You girls are lucky enough to be chosen to serve the legendary Derek Novak himself. That's all I can reveal to you, but one thing I do know for sure is that you can't afford to displease the prince."

She brushed a gentle hand through my hair, arranging it so that it fell perfectly in place.

"But don't worry ... considering how stunning you look, I doubt it will be difficult for you to please him."

She then walked away, making it clear that she wasn't willing to say anything more.

Please him. Shivers ran through my body as questions about my fate began flooding my mind. Being a member of *anyone's* "harem" sounded terrifying to me, but I knew that prying for more answers would most likely lead someone – most likely, myself – into trouble. So, I had to make do with keeping my ears open to the hushed whispers being exchanged around me. All I gathered was that the prince had been asleep for hundreds of years and that "the vampires" see him as some sort of "savior".

I also noted that the women dolling us up were all humans. I wondered if they too had been kidnapped.

Once we were ready, the guards who had escorted us to The Baths came for us. I'll never forget the look on the face of one of the guards when he saw us.

"The prince is one lucky bastard," he muttered under his breath, before instructing us to stand up and follow them.

We were led back along The Vale's cobblestone streets. This time, however, I was too overcome by anxiety to be capable of admiring the town.

It wasn't long before we were led to an exit on a different side of The Vale. We once again found ourselves being herded through a damp forest until we reached another clearing. There was only one structure that presented itself to us – a temple of sorts, with white exterior and a cavern-like roof. Under the moonlight, the whiteness of the building made it shine amidst the black of night.

"Welcome to The Sanctuary, ladies," one of the guards said, a smirk on his face as he ogled us with his amber-gold eyes.

They made us enter the front door. It was in the well-lit corridor in front of us that we saw Lucas and Vivienne. I could feel Lucas' eyes on me, making my insides squirm again. Vivienne instructed us to follow them and we did. We soon turned a corner and walked into a large candlelit chamber.

Standing there, I found myself unable to pry my gaze away from Derek Novak, as I tried to gain some understanding of what all this buzz surrounding him was about.

He was what every teenage girl would describe as *hot*, which was rather ironic considering how pale and frozen he looked. He had the same features as his brother, but there was something more refined about him. There was a hint of boyishness in his face. I could instantly tell that he was younger than Lucas. I entertained the thought that perhaps I was indeed better off under his mercy than Lucas'. However, the words Vivienne had spoken to me earlier that night still haunted me.

"Your best chance at survival and proving your significance is to win Derek's affection… I'm not sure that's even possible."

"What is the meaning of this?! Why would you bring them to me?" Derek spoke up. His voice was deep and powerful as he breathed heavily.

"Take them away from me."

"We can't do that." Vivienne shook her head. "You'll need to learn to control yourself with them. We will give you blood to feed on soon enough, but right now, you need to keep yourself in check when you're around them."

"If you don't want them to die, why bring them to me *now*?!" His voice rumbled through the cavernous hall.

Everything about his demeanor – the way his chest heaved, the way his fists clenched – made it clear that he was doing everything within his power to keep himself from attacking any one of us – perhaps even all of us.

I shuddered at the display of temper from this young man, whose immediate command we were going to be subjected to. Vivienne didn't seem fazed at all. In a calm, collected voice, she responded to her brother.

"Because you and I both know that if you are to face what lies ahead of you, you need to be able to control your impulse to satisfy your hunger. These women were handpicked to become part of your harem. They're the loveliest among a recent hunt."

Lucas chuckled. "This is cruel and unusual punishment, Vivienne. I told you that. Derek hasn't had blood for the past four hundred years. He can't be expected to not want to rip these girls' heads off. Hell, I've been feeding for the last four hundred years and I still want to have my way with them."

Derek, still looking like he was about to attack us at any moment, simply gave him a sideward glare before his eyes roamed toward each of us girls – one by one.

"A harem? A hunt? Since when do we have these? Who are these girls and where exactly did you 'hunt' them?"

Lucas, Vivienne and the other woman present in the hall exchanged uncomfortable glances. It was Vivienne who eventually answered the question.

"They're humans abducted from the outside world. We *hunt* humans to become slaves here, to do the work necessary. Those who prove to be useless are fed on. The choicest and most beautiful among the captives are kept by the Elite as part of what we began calling a *harem* a long time ago. Some of the favored Lodgers also have one or two beauties of their own. The humans who form the harems are kept alive for a year and whoever owns them gets to decide their ultimate fate after that."

"It's really just an excuse to be able to have them at their prime," Lucas added with a smirk.

From the look on Derek's face, he didn't seem pleased about the explanation he'd been given. He eyed us from where he stood – the distance between us was only a few strides.

"I know what you're thinking and no, you can't let them go, Derek," Lucas spoke as if he was talking to a five-year-old. "They've seen The Shade. We can't afford to risk the coven. They stay or they die."

Derek's expression turned to complete disgust. "They can't be any older than we were when we were turned."

"I know," Lucas grinned, speaking as though it were the most amusing fact known to their kind. "They're all seventeen."

"The knights and guards take them at that age, because as you know, blood tastes sweeter once they reach the fullness of their womanhood at eighteen," Vivienne explained.

Lucas scoffed at the notion. "Please. It's all the same, but really, Derek, enjoy them. Just looking at them is already a feast. After the year ends, imagine all the wicked things you can do with them."

Derek stood to his full height – a couple of inches taller than his older brother – and began walking toward us. I held my breath, sure that my knees were about to give way beneath me. I shifted my weight from one foot to the other and in doing so, found the back of my hand brushing against the hand of the blonde-haired girl standing beside me. I could feel her shaking. I grabbed her hand and squeezed it, hoping to both give comfort to and draw it from her.

The motion attracted Derek's attention. I'd never felt more vulnerable than I did the moment Derek Novak's electric blue eyes settled on me. His gaze betrayed the thoughts roaming his mind. I was a lamb – a lamb ready for slaughter.

Chapter 6: Derek

I couldn't pry my eyes away from her. I wanted to stop, but I found myself inching closer.

She was the most beautiful one to behold – not because her physical appearance drew me in above and beyond that of the other girls. No. In my eyes, she was most beautiful because at a time when she had every right to be terrified, she managed to show comfort to another person who needed it.

The moment I saw her grab the hand of the girl beside her, all the others paled in comparison. She showed me a humanity I longed to return to.

But I was the predator. She was my prey. And even as I admired her for that one simple gesture, I was battling to prevent myself from relishing the sweet delicacy she was to my kind.

I muttered several curses under my breath. Vivienne *knew* my struggle to maintain control when it came to satisfying my hunger.

I studied the young woman whose emerald green eyes boldly settled on me. I took in the sight of those dark auburn locks cascading down her shoulders and framing her delicate face. There was an innocence to the slight blush of her freckled cheeks that made me ache inside. Her eyes and the way they were fixed on me – unflinching in their courage and audacity – made me want to shrink away from her.

I knew she was studying me and I would've given anything to find out what was going through her head as she looked me over.

A familiar ache gripped my chest with every step I took closer to her. She was everything I no longer was. She represented everything I lost when my father turned me into this monster.

When I was about two feet away from her, I immediately regretted ever going near her, because the sight and smell of the slightest bit of blood on her lower lip became my complete undoing.

Lightning speed and strength I forgot I had pushed her backward until her back hit one of the sanctuary's giant marble pillars with a loud thud. Guilt and shame filled me for causing her pain, but I was giving in to my nature, desperate to draw her blood and taste it.

I swallowed hard as my eyes centered on the cut on her lip. I knew that the moment I did anything to taste it, I wouldn't be able to control myself. There was no going back.

"Derek, no…"

My uneven breathing and erratic heartbeat drowned out my sister's protests. As far as I was concerned, there was no one else there with us. It was just me and this innocent – this innocent I was about to destroy.

I wrapped an arm around her small waist and lifted her up the pillar, supporting her weight with my hips. She tried to push me away, tried to free herself from my grip, but it didn't take long for her to realize that there was no escape. I was too strong for her and she was at my complete mercy. She knew it. I knew it, and I hated myself, because at that moment, there wasn't a single bit of mercy running through my blood-deprived veins. There was nothing in me but an animalistic and primal need that was begging to be satisfied – *hunger*.

Chapter 7: Sofia

What is it with these people and shoving me up against hard surfaces?

I was fully aware of the gravity of my situation, and yet that was the one thought that circled my mind the moment he lifted me so that my face was directly in front of his. He had me pinned against a black marble pillar. My back was suffering from the abuse it'd been receiving all night long – first from Lucas and now from his brother.

Lucas was right when he referred to me as a "fragile little twig". It was exactly how I felt, with Derek pinning me there, all my attempts to push him away and break free failing miserably. I wasn't even sure if he was aware of how strong he was, but he exuded a power that I didn't sense even with Lucas. I felt like a china doll, as though he could shatter me the moment he wished to.

Everything about Derek Novak was overwhelming my senses. The feel of his tense muscular body pressed against mine, the chill of his breath against my skin, the sound of his uneven breathing, the light scent of his musk mixing with the myrrh they'd applied to my neck back at the spa.

He stared at me and I stared back. I could almost see the wheels in his head turning and every bit of his demeanor showed how conflicted he was about what he wanted to do. And yet, there was also a determination in his sharp blue eyes that left me grasping for any bit of hope.

When his free hand grabbed my head and pushed it to the side to clear my neck as he bared his fangs, all I could think of doing was beg.

"Please ... don't!"

I could hear Vivienne trying to plead with him, reminding him that he could control this. He needed to regain control.

I didn't understand what was going on or why they were doing what they were doing. I just knew that I was at Derek's mercy and yet, unlike what I experienced with Lucas earlier that night, right now nothing about what Derek was doing made me feel violated.

That scared me. This man had me shoved up a hard surface, trapping me with his strong arms, crushing me. He was about to sink his teeth into my bare neck and drink my blood. I had every right to feel violated, but I didn't. *What does that say about me?*

"Derek ... you don't want to do this ... you have control." Vivienne kept shouting.

I looked into Derek's eyes wondering if it was getting to him. It seemed it wasn't, because he pushed against me as he leaned forward, his fangs beginning to press against my neck.

Even as all five of my senses were assailed by sensation after sensation brought about by my predicament, I recalled something Ben always told me when I began to pity myself and blame my circumstances for my sorrow.

"I know an excuse when I hear one, Sofia. Don't you dare dupe yourself into believing that you're the victim."

I tried to push Derek away once again, but surrendered to the idea that it was no use. Instead, I pressed my cheek against his, the warmth of my skin fading into the coldness of his.

"*You can control yourself. Don't do this to me.*" I whispered into his ear.

To my surprise, just when his fangs were about to break my skin and draw blood, he stopped. I could feel the fangs retract until it was just his lips pressed against my neck.

"I can't," he responded hoarsely. "Your blood is too enticing, too sweet..."

Tears began to stream down my face – partly because everything that'd been happening came crashing down on me, overwhelming me, and partly because of how much I ached for Ben as I spoke the same words that he had so many times before.

"*I know an excuse when I hear one. Don't you dare deceive yourself into believing that you're the victim, Derek Novak.*"

I could hear a soft gasp escape his lips the moment I said the words. I sighed with relief when his arm's grip around my waist loosened. His lips remained pressed on any part of my skin they could brush against as he eased me down so I could stand on my feet again. I felt small and fragile standing so close to him. The moment my feet hit the ground, my knees buckled and to my horror, I found myself leaning against him for support. He slipped his arm around me and propped me up.

"You'll be alright," he whispered loud enough for only me to hear.

I wanted to throw a bitter, sarcastic retort at him. *How could he say something like that after what he almost did to me?* I found, however, that I had no energy left in me to put up a fight.

His eyes were still on me as he spoke. "Tell me your name."

"Sofia… Sofia Claremont."

He then began to speak louder, now addressing everyone else in the room.

"Sofia is to be my personal slave."

"And the others?" Vivienne asked.

Derek didn't even look at them.

"You decide."

Other words were exchanged, but I did not hear them. The thought circling my head was overwhelmingly sickening.

What exactly does he mean by "personal slave"?

Chapter 8: Derek

Four hundred years. Gone. Just like that.

As Lucas and Vivienne led me out of the Sanctuary, apparently Corrine's dwelling place, I couldn't help but marvel over what they'd managed to turn The Shade into over the past four centuries. Before the spell, the island we'd occupied and called The Shade was nothing but a fortress surrounded by a dark forest with its towering sequoias. We made a small clearing in the middle of the forest and called it The Vale. That was where we began making plans for what The Shade would become. I never thought it possible for most of those plans to actually materialize, but here it was — right before my very eyes — more amazing than it had been in my imagination.

As we left the Sanctuary and eventually entered into what was now the Vale, I asked question after question to satisfy my curiosity and make me forget my hunger. Sofia and the other slaves were walking right behind us, escorted by the guards. I was still so conscious of Sofia's proximity, still allured by the scent of her blood.

"What happened to the wild animals that occupied the forest?" I asked.

We'd made plans to keep our residences atop the redwoods, because of what a nuisance the wildlife had turned out to be.

"They're around," Vivienne explained as we took a leisurely pace strolling past the Vale. "Cora helped us gather most of the wild animals into certain parts of the island we call *dens*. Some of the fiercer ones, however, are kept in the Cells."

"The Cells?"

"The prisons," Lucas butted in. "They're located in the Black Heights – you know," he shrugged, "the mountain ranges. The dungeons and slave quarters are kept there."

I raised a brow. "Sofia?"

I didn't miss how Vivienne's eyes shot toward me in question. I knew she was intrigued by the concern I was showing for the girl. At that time, there was no way for me to explain to my sister exactly how I saw Sofia: a ray of light. The truth was I didn't even fully understand myself.

"Harems stay at the Residences with their keepers," Vivienne explained, assuring me that Sofia wasn't going anywhere without me.

I nodded. "And what exactly are the Residences?"

"You'll find out soon enough. That's where we're going." Lucas said. There was a certain smugness to my brother's tone. I imagined he was pleased that he had four hundred years' worth of experience and knowledge over me.

I stared back and forth from my sister to my brother, wondering about the amount of knowledge and wisdom they'd managed to accumulate over all that time. I didn't know if it was my bias against my brother or the fact that we were never close due to how our father always pitted us against each other, but Lucas didn't seem to be any wiser than he was when I went under Cora's spell. Vivienne, on the other hand, had a sager aura about her and I couldn't help but feel some sort of reverence toward her.

I then began to wonder where my father was. The fact that I had no pressing desire to see him told me a lot about my feelings toward him. I immediately assumed that he'd be in the Crimson Fortress, the massive walls I made sure would be built to protect The Shade before I sought escape. I found myself asking to verify if the fortress was still standing strong and if Oliver, always the fierce warrior, was there.

"The fortress is stronger than ever. We have knights, guards and scouts stationed at its walls to keep us all secure," Vivienne assured.

"Knights? Scouts?"

"Knights are members of the Elite who also serve as warriors," Lucas explained. "Scouts are those we send to the outside world for supplies or new blood."

I wasn't sure how I felt about that last piece of information. I'd always pondered over whether there was a way for our kind to survive without preying on humans. I was sure that just saying those thoughts out loud would be labeled as sacrilege by my father.

"And father?"

"He's meeting with leaders from the other covens to discuss how to stop the damned hunters once and for all," Vivienne explained.

My jaw tightened at the mention of the hunters dedicated to ending our kind. I remembered a time when I was one of them. That was long ago.

"They're still a threat?" I asked.

"More than ever before," Lucas said, almost sounding indignant that I didn't know – as if it were my fault that the hunters were so powerful. "We're the strongest and most powerful coven remaining. A lot of the citizens of The Shade – Lodgers we call them – escaped from covens that the hunters managed to find and completely annihilate."

Vivienne most likely sensed my agitation over the news, because she quickly changed the subject. "The hunters are a topic for a later date." She said, curtly.

We had just reached the outskirts of The Vale and were now about to enter a different part of the redwood forest. I admired how much The Shade had changed. Before the spell, it could barely be called a community. It was our escape, our safe sanctuary from the hunters, who were threatening to expel every single one of our kind from the earth.

If I didn't have my father, brother and sister to fight for, I would've surrendered myself to the hunters, ending my life under their cruel hands. But at the time, I couldn't bear to do it to my family, especially not to Vivienne. The coven needed me, but once I had fulfilled my part of the bargain and managed to bring them to this safe haven, winning Cora over to our side for protection, I knew I couldn't bear to live another second with all the blood that was on my hands. I had to end it.

But I was a coward. I dreaded to think of what would happen once I actually died. *What happens to the living dead once they pass away?* I shuddered every time I found myself thinking about it. It was perhaps quite a strange thing that the undead could be so afraid of death, and yet it was true.

I was afraid to die, so I went to sleep instead.

As we walked through the dense wood, I spoke my thoughts. "You must hate me for having done what I did ... abandoning you all."

I noticed how Lucas' jaw twitched, a flicker of the familiar resentment showing in his eyes. I didn't need to hear a response from him to know what was going through his mind. He hated me.

Vivienne was far more gracious. "No, Derek. You did what had to be done to protect us all without even knowing it. Your rested state has caused you to gain energy over the hundreds of years that you were under Cora's spell. Because of this, you're most likely the strongest and most powerful vampire in existence today."

Vivienne's words echoed through my head … *strongest and most powerful vampire.* Recollections of how I practically threw Sofia up that pillar roamed through my mind.

My gut clenched. She looked fragile under my grasp and yet so fearless. I was death and I was looking her right in the eye. She looked right back, barely flinching. She was walking behind me. I could hear her gentle footsteps and the clanging of the shackles on her wrists. I could still smell and practically taste the blood on her lips. I wondered if this was the same effect women had on me before. I couldn't remember.

I stopped in my tracks and called to her. "Sofia."

Everyone else stopped walking the moment I spoke.

Her youth showed in the way she responded to me. "*What?*"

Without even looking back, I knew that she was about to suffer pain for her insolence in addressing me. The guard behind us was raising his hand to hit her.

"Don't touch her," I said. "Sofia, walk beside me."

Everyone held their breath at the momentary silence that followed. I could sense her thinking, weighing the pros and cons of what could happen should she dare defy me. Then the shackles began clinking as she stepped forward to fill the empty spot by my side.

I didn't dare look at her. Having her so close was already taking its toll on my self-control… I was certain that just the sight of the warm blush on her cheeks would remind me of her blood and my longing to partake of it.

"Get rid of these restraints. She has nowhere to run to."

"Brother…" Vivienne began to protest. "If she uses the freedom you're giving her to raise a hand against you, you might not be able to control yourself from…"

"I won't feed on her." I said it with more conviction and self-assurance than I felt. "Do as I say and remove the chains."

My command was obeyed immediately. It was yet another reminder of who I was before, of how much they all feared me. I waited until the restraints were removed before I took a first step forward, the group following my pace.

Lucas and Vivienne tried to make conversation as we trekked through the dark wood, but I was no longer paying attention. I was too distracted by Sofia, aware of every single one of her actions. She rubbed her wrists as she observed her surroundings. She was taking in every detail, her bright eyes showing fear mixed with mild fascination. Before I could keep myself from doing it, I grabbed her hand, my fingers intertwining with hers.

She flinched at my touch. I knew I had no right to take that sort of liberty with her, but I gave myself the indulgence, because I really just wanted to feel her warmth.

I could only guess what was going through her mind, because at some point, she squeezed my hand like she did to that other girl back in the Sanctuary. She couldn't have known how much that meant to me.

Chapter 9: Sofia

His hand was so cold. A chill climbed from the hand he was holding all the way up to my elbow. I couldn't understand why he would do that – hold my hand. But the gesture strangely brought me comfort where I had none.

As we took that walk to wherever it was that the Prince's quarters were situated, I kept my eyes open for a means of escape. We'd just left the Vale and were now being ushered into another creepy wood, though I was sure that some other clearing would come to view, showing us another aspect of The Shade that would astound my imagination.

At this point, however, there was nothing to be seen, but the same monotonous sights afforded by a dark forest, lit only by the torch flames the guards were carrying; tall trees with their long, foreboding branches, rocks lining the side of the dirt pathway, thorny thickets scattered here and there.

My thoughts roamed back to the people I saw back at the Vale. It was easy to tell the difference between the vampires and humans. The vampires wore designer outfits that looked like they were taken straight out of the pages of Vogue. I had always imagined vampires wearing black tight-fitting leather or long dark trench coats. Not these ones. Humans, on the other hand, had a uniform – gray cotton overalls for the men, white cotton smocks for the women.

It was evident that most of the work was being done by the humans, while the vampires appeared to be taking leisurely strolls around the place or spending time with each other – most of them having a human or two trailing behind them, ready to cater to their slightest whims. I was fairly certain that we humans were the workforce that was keeping The Shade going. We were The Shade's blood and sweat.

I remembered a particular scene I'd witnessed while we were being dragged past the Vale. From a distance, I saw a vampire hit a young man across the face, causing the boy to crash to the ground. I wanted to run there and do something about it. Even in high school, I made it clear to Ben and all of our friends that I would never stand for bullying.

Of course, there was no way for me to do anything about what I saw here. I was chained behind the vampires and guarded like a wild animal. I hated how helpless I felt and found myself squeezing Derek's hand. It was mostly caused by instinct, like an impulse reaction to the memory, but when I realized what I'd done and looked at Derek for a reaction, I could swear I saw gratefulness in his sharp blue eyes.

"We're here." Vivienne announced, stopping abruptly in the middle of the forest. "Welcome to the Pavilion, Derek."

I frowned and looked around. I could only see the dark silhouettes of thick tree trunks.

Derek seemed just as confused as I was.

"Hm? I don't understand…"

Lucas smirked. "Was it not your bloody suggestion to build the Residences on top of trees?"

Before his comment could even register in my mind, Lucas leaped upward. I looked up toward the sky. What I saw made my head spin. My mouth dropped open.

Glowing atop the giant redwoods were networks of tree houses. Although from what I could see from the ground, to merely call them tree houses, would be a grave injustice.

They were modern, high-end villas connected from one tree to another by glass-covered walkways and hanging bridges. How it was possible for them to build those things up there was beyond my comprehension, but there they were – luxurious villas built on trees. The very thought of going up there began triggering my non-existent fear of heights.

My amazement was momentarily interrupted when I saw the reaction on Derek's face. His eyes had softened as he gazed up at "The Residences" with unveiled awe.

He then shifted his attention to his sister and with a practically broken voice, said, "You remembered."

Vivienne smiled. "How could I forget?"

I stood there, witnessing this trace of affection and humanity between them. For a moment, I actually felt jealous of what Derek and Vivienne had. I could see how much they doted on each other.

No words were uttered next, because no words were necessary. They understood, and in a strange way, so did I. Vivienne leaped into the air just as Lucas had done moments before. That's when I realized that there were no stairs. Not even a ladder in sight. I opened my mouth, wondering how on earth I was going to get up there, but before words could come out, I saw a glint of amusement spark in the corners of Derek's eyes.

He didn't bother to ask my permission. He simply wrapped his strong arms around my waist and pulled me against him. Before I could prepare myself for what was about to happen, he took a vertical leap that left my mind whirling as I gasped for breath, instinctively wrapping my arms around his neck and clinging to him for dear life.

When I felt him pull away from me and settle my feet on what felt like hardwood flooring, I dared open my eyes.

After I'd recovered from the shock, now that I was closer to the buildings, I could fully marvel at their beauty. The villas came in different styles, most of them having only one floor, but some having two. They were the kind you would find in five-star beach resorts with their large glass windows and a tropical feel to the architectural design; the kind you would see in some exotic location. The only difference was these just happened to perch on top of trees towering hundreds of feet off the ground.

I walked toward the edge of a wide terrace and found myself overlooking one of the most magnificent scenes I'd ever laid eyes on. It was more beautiful than a painting. Thousands of glittering stars were peppered across the pitch-black canvas that was the sky. These stars and the full moon's beams were the only light to grace the landscape.

I dared not look directly downward. I preferred not to scare myself by discovering just how high up we were. But I could tell that this was one of the tallest trees on the whole island. A massive sea of black treetops sprawled out beneath me for miles. And, looming far in the distance were mountains. Mountains so high the tops were capped with white. I could only imagine how stunning this place would be at sunrise.

I tasted salt as a cool sea wind suddenly whipped across my face. What unsettled me was, despite how high up I was standing, I could not see any end to the forest. No sign of the shore. Not even the faintest clue in which direction I would run even if I managed to get free from Derek's grasp. I gasped.

"It's beautiful, isn't it?" Derek thought I was gasping with pleasure. His voice was husky.

I just nodded as I leaned my weight over the wooden banister that lined the terrace, trying to distract my mind from the writhing I now felt within my stomach.

I began wondering about the other girls we'd left behind and figured that the guards would take care of them. I wasn't sure whether the favor Derek was showing me was to my advantage or not. Somehow, I felt far more secure with the other girls around.

Whatever had become of them, I didn't have a choice but to move on according to Derek's pace, because he once again grabbed my hand and pulled me along as Vivienne and Lucas led us both to his quarters.

"This is one of four penthouses that comprise The Pavilion, which was built specifically for our family," Vivienne explained as she unlocked the oak door of the lavish penthouse with large glass windows. "There's one for each of us – you, father, Lucas and I."

Even as we moved toward the tree house, I stared at the giant windows in wonder. If what I knew about vampires was correct, wouldn't they object to all the sunlight that would stream right through?

I gave the vampires surrounding me wary glances; that I should stand amidst them like it was the most normal thing jolted me to attention. No matter how awed I was by The Shade's beauty, I had to remember that I was there against my will. I couldn't trust any of them – not Lucas, not Vivienne, and especially not Derek.

Where there's a way in, there simply must be a way out.

I paid close attention to what the home looked like from the inside. Indoors, the penthouse looked even more massive. We were ushered into what I assumed was the living room based on the furniture it sported – a large flat screen TV, a fireplace, abstract art on the smooth cream walls, plush black leather couches … it wasn't exactly how I would picture Count Dracula's abode.

My eyes circled the room and noticed that there were three entry-ways surrounding it – aside from the one we entered. At each entry-way were glass doors that led to more glass-covered walkways leading to other rooms of the penthouse.

"And the Elite live where?" Derek asked, seemingly satisfied by what he saw.

"The other Elites live in the Penthouses –tree houses similar to the ones we have, but ours, of course," Lucas smirked, "are far more luxurious, because let's face it: a Novak deserves only the best."

When he said *the best,* he eyed me pointedly and I found myself backing up a step, but Derek's firm grip on my hand kept me from going too far. It was almost as if he wanted me anchored to him. I couldn't understand why. I looked at him, wondering what he intended to do to me that night. The thoughts roaming around my head made me shudder.

"The Pavilion's penthouses have more rooms than I can keep track of," Vivienne said.

"There's the living room, the dining room, the kitchen, a library, several baths, an indoor pool, an entertainment room, a theater, a master bedroom, several guestrooms and your harem's quarters. There are several rooms that we left untouched, just in case you think of something you wish to do with them."

"A music room," Derek said immediately.

My eyebrows rose in surprise. I never would have expected that he was musically inclined.

Vivienne smiled. "Of course. I'll see to it that the scouts get everything you need. Do you want me to show you to your bedroom?"

Derek shook his head. "I'll manage."

My heart sank. The thought of me being alone with him in that place was unnerving. I tried to pull my hand away from his grasp, but he held on tight.

Vivienne seemed to take notice of this, but paid it no heed. Instead, she walked toward her brother and gave him a hug. Finally, he let go of my hand in order to reciprocate her gesture.

I stepped backward. That's when I noticed Lucas staring at the hand Derek just let go of. He looked like he wanted to crush it. I balled my fists and hid them behind the silky fabric of the exquisite dress they'd made me wear. I felt Lucas' eyes on me, traveling along every curve of my body. I wanted to bolt away.

"It's only a few hours until morning. We'd best get going," Vivienne said. "I'll instruct the guards to have the girls brought to their quarters … unless you have other plans."

Derek shook his head. "Take them there. Except for Sofia. She stays in the bedroom nearest mine."

Vivienne gave me a pointed look, as if she was wondering what was so special about me. That made two of us.

She nodded. "Very well. See you tomorrow, Derek."

The moment they closed the door behind them, I wanted to back away from Derek but found myself rooted to the spot. He turned around, studying his surroundings until his gaze fell on me.

"You're just standing there," he remarked.

I shrugged. "I have nowhere to go, do I?"

"Why are you not afraid of me?" He began to draw closer.

I wanted to run – the same way I should have when Lucas first approached me on the beach.

"What *on earth* makes you think I'm not afraid of you?"

"I thought maybe you're one of those girls."

"Which girls?"

"Girls who are fascinated by our kind," he stopped a few steps away from me, almost as if he were afraid to draw closer. "Girls who want to be like us."

"I can describe your kind in many words," I practically spat out. "*Fascinating* isn't one of them. Is that really what you think you are? Fascinating?"

He took a step back, almost as if he was hurt by my words. He shook his head, a bitter smile forming on his lips.

"No. Far from it."

"Why am I here? What are you going to do with me?" The questions came out of my lips before I could stop them. The tone of desperation in my voice was evident.

He stared as if he were battling with himself whether to answer my questions or not.

"Go to sleep, Sofia." He said finally. "You need the rest."

My heart sank.

"You're not going to let me go, are you?"

He shook his head.

"No. I can't let you go. You've seen too much."

I gritted my teeth. *No way am I going to stay here forever.* I had every intention of escaping and I figured the morning would be the best time to do it. As we both found our way to the other rooms and discovered where our bedrooms were, I had one thought circling my mind: I had to escape by daybreak.

I guess I underestimated The Shade when it came to its penchant for surprises. I drifted off to sleep in a round comfortable bed covered with furs, expecting to see sunlight breaking through the bedroom windows the next morning. To my horror, I woke up to a deep, dark night.

Chapter 10: Derek

The moment I laid myself down on the covers of the four poster bed in the middle of the lavish bedroom I'd chosen for myself, the first thought that came to mind was: *What on earth are you doing?* I'd just woken up from four centuries of sleep. There really was no more sleeping to be done. Thus, I spent the night in the library, reading books – hoping to catch up with what I'd missed over the past few centuries. I found a wealth of information there, but I knew that I'd only scratched the surface. I then realized how valuable Sofia would be to me in becoming acquainted with the world as it was now.

I picked up the fourth glass of blood that was brought to me by one of the harem girls. A gift from Vivienne.

When the girl, Gwen, tentatively came in with the first glass, I didn't even care to ask where the blood came from or whose blood it was. I just drank it all up. My hunger had to be satisfied if I were to keep myself from murdering the girls who were living inside my home. I thanked her for the blood and asked if she could fetch me more. The blonde nodded, her lips trembling even as she moved away from me. I looked at her and wondered why I wasn't as drawn to her as I was to Sofia. It could be said that she was similarly pleasant to look at as the redhead sleeping in the chambers next to mine, and yet that simple gesture of Sofia back at the Sanctuary – grabbing Gwen's hand to comfort her – somehow solidified Sofia, in my eyes, as more valuable than all the other girls combined.

As I finished my fourth glass, I found myself longing to check on how my beautiful captive was doing. I stood up and made my way through a glass-covered walkway which displayed the starlit sky above. I smiled. It was a nice touch by Cora – always keeping the sun out of The Shade – the one place on earth where it was always night.

I eventually ended up outside her bedroom. I drew a sharp breath. I couldn't understand why I was so nervous. She was just a girl. *I've had my fill of blood.* There was no reason to be so anxious. I knocked on the door and waited. *Nothing.* I knocked again.

"Sofia?"

Something was wrong. I opened the door. It wasn't locked. For some reason, that bothered me. *Is she so foolish to trust a stranger like me – a vampire at that – that she wouldn't even lock her door?* I pushed the door open and surveyed the room. She was nowhere in sight.

"Sofia?" I stepped in, the truth beginning to dawn on me.

I was the fool to trust her. I didn't even bother to station guards outside her bedroom. Of course she would attempt to escape. She'd be a fool if she didn't.

Chapter 11: Sofia

Run, Sofia. I kept telling myself to go on, to flee. I figured that at some point, I'd reach something – anything – to give me a clue on how I could escape The Shade. And so I continued, stumbling through the darkness of the forest.

I knew I had no escape plan and the likelihood of actually leaving the island was practically non-existent. But I had to take my chance the moment I saw it. I couldn't afford to hang around while Derek decided exactly what he wanted to keep me for.

I thought of Ben and what he would do given my situation. Knowing how impulsive my best friend was, I figured to escape while he could was probably what he would've done. That really was all the encouragement I needed. So when I woke up that morning – and found the sky to be as dark as it was the night before – I realized that waiting for daylight to escape would mean waiting forever.

I slipped myself out of bed as quietly as I could – I had no idea where Derek was, but if he was in the chambers closest to mine, I figured he'd hear every single noise that I made, so I took care in making none. I removed the slippers I'd found in the large wardrobe within the bedroom. I figured I'd make less noise with bare feet.

I quietly sifted through the closet which I discovered mostly contained women's clothes. It made my stomach turn as I thought about it. The idea that the room next to Derek's was specifically meant for a woman – and what that woman could possibly be intended for – made me feel sick. Whatever reasons these vampires had for taking us, what they were doing was horrific.

I wasn't just going to sit there and be the victim.

I tried to look for jeans or something comfortable to run in, but found none. My hands sifted through dozens of silken gowns, cocktail dresses, skirts and French lingerie.

Eventually I found a pair of denim shorts and a black hoodie two sizes too large for me. I frowned, noting how out-of-place the outfit was considering the rest of the contents of the wardrobe. I shrugged it off, just thankful that I no longer had to sprint through a dark forest in a tight cocktail dress. I put the clothes on as quickly as I could. I knew there was no time to waste.

The further I got without anyone noticing I was gone, the better off I'd be.

Satisfied with my outfit, I snuck outside the room, carrying the rubber slippers I had with one hand, careful to close the door as noiselessly as I could. I made my way toward one of the glass-covered walkways connecting the corridor outside the guest room, to another wing of the penthouse.

Standing in the walkway, I saw one of the human girls travelling along the walkway parallel to where I was standing, all the way to the wing on the opposite side. She was the one whose hand I held when we were first brought in front of Derek. I couldn't remember her name. My hopes lifted. If she was there, perhaps Derek was also. I thought for a moment if I should include the other girls in my escape. I wanted to, but I figured it would be a case of the blind leading the blind. My best chance of helping them was to escape and expose The Shade to the rest of the world. Surely someone would help me save the people brought into this coven as slaves.

I didn't spend too much time musing over this and instead, focused on how the hell I was going to get back to the ground. I looked outside and smiled faintly with relief. I saw an elevator not too far away. *That must be it.* I pulled the black hoodie over my head and crept toward the narrow metal doors. It didn't take long before my feet were back on the solid ground. It was almost too good to be true, but no one seemed to be around to keep watch over me, so I just put the slippers on and ran toward the direction opposite the Vale. I figured that north of the Vale were the Cells, east of it was the Sanctuary, while on the west side was the Pavilion. If I ran in the direction away from the Vale, further to the west, I just had to reach an exit sooner or later.

Where there's a way in, there must be a way out.

I was so wrong. After what felt like hours of staggering through the gloomy forest - with the rubber slippers blistering my feet and getting completely battered by the sharp twigs and stones - every muscle in my body was aching and I had scratches all over arms and legs due to branches I hit, or bushes I stumbled into due to the severe lack of lighting. I finally reached a clearing leading out of what had seemed like an endless forest.

But what I saw made my heart sink. Before me stood a wall so tall and wide, I was surprised no one had ever noticed The Shade on a map before. *This would give the Wall of China a run for its money.* I frowned. How I planned to get past this wall, I had no clue, and the fact that I had no idea what was on the other side of it didn't help either.

I bit my lip, unsure of what to do. I sank to the ground, fighting the urge to break down and cry. There was no way I could climb this wall. My feet were so sore, I could barely stand up. I was beginning to grow desperate. The thought of returning and facing the consequences of my botched escape was playing tricks on my mind. I was overwhelmed by more fears and doubts than I knew how to handle.

Suddenly, I heard a twig snap behind me.

"Well, what do we have here? Look, Husky!" Spoke a voice that was a tad too high-pitched for a man.

A deeper, huskier voice replied. "Looks like dinner to me, Pitchy."

My fists clenched and I scrambled to my feet. I was suddenly aware of how many scratches I had and the blood that was oozing from those scrapes. I'd turned myself into bait for these creatures, who had just stepped out from the shadows of the trees and were swiftly approaching me. Based on the clothes the vampires were wearing – black garb with red crests worn by the guards escorting us the night before – I assumed both of them were guards, assigned to keep watch over the fortress.

"What are you doing way out here by the fortress during a night so dark?" Pitchy asked.

"Taking a walk. My master said I could," I bluffed. I could feel my face turning red.

"Really now?" This time, it was Husky speaking. "Did he also ask you to get yourself all bloody and ready to become his breakfast while you're at it?"

"Who's your master, lovely little thing?" Pitchy was right beside me now.

He reached out and grabbed a clump of my hair within his fingers, taking a good long sniff. I was about to tell them that Derek Novak owned me and harming me would be a big mistake, but was interrupted by Husky before I could speak.

"Who cares?" he spoke up. "Anyone who walks past the forest and reaches the fortress is at our mercy. I'm sure her master will thank us for teaching the insolent slave a lesson."

His finger traced one of the scratches on my legs, drawing blood with his protruding claw. I whimpered with pain. He took a whiff of the blood and smiled before tasting it.

"Sweet."

It was Pitchy who seemed apprehensive: "Perhaps we shouldn't touch her. We don't know who owns her." Still, his eyes were on me, his free hand running the length of my arm.

Husky showed no indication of stopping his tasting tests of the blood coming out of the scrapes on my body. I stood there, trying to recall whatever it was I learned from the self-defense lessons Ben had convinced me to take part in. I had no idea if they would work on vampires, but it was worth a try – if only just to stun them so I could make a run for it. I bent down on the ground and swung a leg beneath Husky, making him topple to the ground. I took advantage of Pitchy's surprise and pushed him away before I turned back toward the forest. I had barely taken four strides, before both managed to catch up with me, dragging me to the ground.

Pitchy held my arms down, while Husky knelt on the ground to hold my feet.

"That was a big mistake, sugar," Husky grinned.

Both their fangs came out and I was sure I was about to lose all sanity, considering that it was the third time in the past twenty-four hours that vampires had threatened to suck my blood.

I saw no hope whatsoever and shut my eyes as both were about to bite. I was expecting to scream in pain upon feeling their fangs dig into me.

But, instead, I felt their grip on my wrists and legs suddenly loosen.

I opened my eyes and blinked several times, still trying to get used to seeing in the dark. My eyes lit up when I saw both guards on the ground with Derek looming over them. The moon shone down on him in the clearing. Both his hands were pinning them to position by their necks.

"Has either one of you tasted her blood?" Derek demanded, the tone of his voice nothing short of menacing.

From behind, the way his shoulders rose with every breath and the way his muscles bulged told me that he was desperately trying to maintain a grip over his temper.

"Your highness, I-I... I didn't mean to..." Husky was shaking so badly I could barely make out his words. "I didn't know..."

What happened next was unlike anything I'd witnessed even in the most ghastly nightmare. Derek let go of Husky's neck and without a single moment's hesitation, dug his claws into Husky's chest. I heard the sound of flesh breaking as Derek ripped out Husky's bloody still-beating heart. My knees weakened at the sight and I fell to the ground. Derek then turned on Pitchy who was shrieking out hysterical apologies.

"Be silent," Derek ordered.

Pitchy lost no time in shutting his mouth and sparing us the annoying sound of his voice.

"Never touch what's mine. *Sofia Claremont is mine.* Whoever harms her answers to *me*. Understood?" Derek growled.

Pitchy nodded. "Of course, y-your M-Majesty."

Derek let go of Pitchy's throat and the guard scampered away from the prince. Derek tossed the then very much dead heart he was holding with his right hand to the ground. He then wiped Husky's blood off his hands using the dead guard's shirt. He rose to his feet and turned, his eyes settling on me. I thought of backing away from him, but saw its futility. He was glaring at me and I found myself fearing his anger.

"Get up, Sofia."

I quickly rose my feet. I was expecting to experience some form of pain. Instead, I found him looking at the length of my legs, concerned by the scratches he saw there. He brought out a dagger he had hidden up his sleeve. I stared at it, wondering if he was going to use it to teach me a lesson of sorts. Instead, he cut through his palm with it.

Despite my fear of him, I stepped forward, momentarily concerned.

"What are you doing?" My eyes were glued to the deep red blood now spilling from his palm – his blood.

"You shouldn't have done what you did," was all the response I got. He lifted his palm, directing it toward my mouth. "Drink."

My eyes grew wide open as I stared at his dirty bloody palm. I gulped, disgusted.

"Ugh, I can't!"

"You *will*. It will heal your scrapes," he insisted. "Marching you back to the Residences with all those bloody scratches will only make you a walking target for every vampire we pass by."

I gave him an incredulous look, wondering if he too wanted to drink my blood at that moment. Tears were beginning to moisten my eyes, but I knew from the look on his face that we weren't going to leave that spot until I did what he was telling me to do.

"Drink, Sofia," he repeated – more sternly this time, impatience obvious in the tone of his voice. "My palm will heal in just a couple of seconds. Don't make me cut myself again."

I once again looked at his palm, unable to believe what I was about to do. I held his wrist with one hand, his fingers with the other. I noticed how his jaw twitched the moment I touched him. I gulped before doing the unthinkable – I began sucking the blood off his palm until his self-inflicted gash closed. I stepped back, the strange taste of his blood overwhelming my taste buds. For a few seconds, I had to fight the urge to puke.

"Good," he said, as he wiped off the thick red liquid dripping from the corners of my mouth with his sleeve.

I checked the gashes I had on my legs. Just like he said, all of them had gone. I still could not wrap my mind around the fact that I just drank blood, a vampire's blood. I didn't even think they *had* their own blood. I was aware of how badly I was trembling.

Derek inched closer to me and brushed his thumb against my cheekbone. His eyes were filled with concern.

"Are you alright?"

I stood still, my eyes drawn to the guard's corpse on the ground.

"You killed him," I said, betraying how stunned I felt. "Just like that ... he's dead."

Derek heaved a deep sigh, a stoic expression taking over his face.

"I had to make an example of him. The other guard will make it known to the entire coven that you are not to be harmed because of what I did. You're safer that way. Besides, he'd tasted your blood. He had to die."

I still looked at him with a stunned expression on my face.

"*He was going to kill you.* He'd tasted your blood, Sofia. I doubt he would've had enough self-control to keep himself from devouring you completely." He raised his left eyebrow, his mood lightening up a bit. "From the expression on your face as they were both about to sink their teeth into you, I'm certain you knew that you wouldn't be able to talk them out of supping on you, as you did with me."

Recollections of the previous night flowed through my mind. I remembered how conflicted Derek seemed as he raised me up against that pillar. There was no conflict of that sort evident in the vampire he just killed.

I found myself intrigued by Derek – even more so than I was before. He was a paradox, a walking contradiction. How he could perform such a violent act without hesitation in one moment, and be as gentle as he was with me in the next, was something that left me unnerved.

I could sense his eyes traveling the length of my body.

"You've been running for hours, haven't you?" he concluded.

I almost felt embarrassed to admit it. "It feels like it."

"Even if you get past the wall, you're on an island, Sofia. Unless you can swim for miles, past the sharks, and get back to the mainland, there's no way out of here."

Before I could respond to that, he scooped me up in his arms and in a matter of minutes, we were back at his Penthouse. He carried me to my bedroom and laid me on the bed.

"We'll have breakfast in half an hour. Have a bath and get dressed in something other than *that*," he looked at my outfit pointedly. It dawned on me that considering the time he'd been asleep, he'd probably never seen a lady wearing a hoodie and shorts before.

Before he turned toward the door, he asked, "Is there anything you need, Sofia?"

I need to get out of here was what I wanted to say.

Instead, I shook my head. "No."

He nodded and headed for the door. He stopped just as he was about to open it. He locked eyes with me and gave one final warning.

"You will only risk your life trying to escape, Sofia. So let's make this simple. Don't *ever* try again."

Chapter 12: Derek

Despite my efforts not to, I kept staring. I was seated at the table, watching her as she made her way around the kitchen in a light yellow dress that perfectly complemented her figure. She was making her breakfast – two pieces of bread that she stuck in a contraption she called a toaster. She retrieved a bottle of strawberry jam and a slab of butter from the "two-door refrigerator," which was apparently a cooling closet for food.

As she began dabbing butter over one piece of bread, her green eyes rose to meet mine. She stopped what she was doing and stared for a couple of seconds.

I found it rather unsettling to have her look at me that way. I couldn't understand why. *She's just a girl, Novak. When have you ever been so riled up over one girl?*

"What?" I said.

"Thank you… for rescuing me. I was pretty sure those guards

were going to turn me into their breakfast."

I didn't answer. She was my responsibility. It was my duty to see to her safety.

"I'm sorry you were taken away from life outside. I understand all this must be traumatic," I said.

She focused on preparing her breakfast, though her long lashes fluttered at my apology.

After a pause, she spoke up. "I can't make this clear enough. No matter what you think, I'm not *yours*, Derek. You told the guard that I was yours. I'm *not*."

I admired her boldness. She was talking to me like she would an equal, never holding back from speaking her mind and yet she managed to pull it off with a feminine grace I found charming and rather off-putting. I debated with myself whether I should address her statements. As far as everyone at The Shade was concerned, she was mine. It was just the simple truth and no matter how she would like to believe otherwise, it remained true. I sighed and let it go. *Let her believe what she will.*

"It's never morning here. Why is that?" She changed the subject, perhaps realizing that she wasn't going to get a response from me.

"A witch's spell keeps the sunlight away." I looked out of the window. "Here at The Shade, it's forever night. I haven't seen the sun in five hundred years."

When I looked up at her, I was taken aback by the expression in her eyes. It felt like she was seeing through me, studying me.

"You're five hundred years old?" She asked after a pause, seemingly satisfied by whatever it was that she saw in me.

I shook my head. "I'm eighteen. I will forever be eighteen."

"That's how old you were when you... *turned*?"

I nodded.

"Who turned you?"

Unnerved by the barrage of questions, digging up unwanted memories, I stood up and looked her straight in the eye.

"Let's have breakfast now, shall we." I said, bluntly.

I was relieved that she didn't pry further. She picked up her plate and headed off with me to the dining area. I smiled when I found a glass of blood already waiting at the table for me.

She stared at it even as she took her seat.

I found myself amused by the expression on her face as I sat across the table from her, taking a sip from the glass. Sofia watched, her eyes wide with a mix of fascination and horror.

"I'll never get used to this," she muttered.

"Get used to what?" a deep voice asked from one corner of the room.

Her eyes shot toward the direction of the voice, but I didn't need to look to know who it was.

"Lucas." I said, flatly.

"You killed a vampire – a guard at that." Lucas eyed Sofia curiously. "For *her*."

"You've heard."

"Pitchy has been squeaking about it all morning." Lucas took a seat beside Sofia.

It didn't take a lot of perception to see that she was uncomfortable around him. Knowing my brother, I wouldn't have been surprised if he had tried to pull something with her.

Lucas set his eyes on her as he laid an arm over the back of her seat.

"So what makes Sofia – stunning as she is – worth the life of one of our own, Derek?"

"She's *mine*," I repeated, giving Sofia a pointed look. "The guard assaulted her, tasted her blood. He had it coming."

My brother's face twitched at the mention of the guard having tasted Sofia's blood. The reaction awakened my curiosity. *Does he want Sofia?*

"I see how that could've been a problem. This one has something about her that just makes us vamps crave her." Lucas' gaze traveled from her face to her neck. "The pathetic loser wouldn't have been able to resist."

The lust was unmistakable. He was practically undressing her with those eyes and I could tell that Sofia felt it based on how she sat there tense and unmoving. I wanted to tackle my brother to the ground, but was certain that it would only serve to earn Sofia his ire.

"Why are you here, Lucas?"

That effectively snapped his attention back to me.

"As much as I would like to say that I missed having you around, little brother, I really didn't." He sighed. "Vivienne asked that we meet. No better time than today to let you know what you're up against now that you're awake."

"What exactly am I up against?" I leant back in my seat as I took another sip from my glass. "And where is Vivienne?"

"Busy doing heaven-knows-what." Lucas fished for something in his pocket and threw it my way. I caught it and stared at it. It looked like a metal slate of sorts. What it was for, I had no idea.

"What is *this*?"

"It's a cell phone. You use it to call people, text them. A communication device." He once again laid his eyes on Sofia. "I'm sure your teenage lovely here is perfectly capable of teaching you how to use it."

He brushed the back of his hand against Sofia's cheek and she immediately flinched at his touch. Of course, that only amused

Lucas. The moment I saw this, an unmistakable fury boiled up within me. I tried to control my temper.

"I'd appreciate that you not touch her. As I already made clear this morning, I do not like it when others mess with what is mine." There was an edge to my voice – one that my brother was very familiar with. The amused expression on Lucas' face disappeared and the atmosphere immediately became tense.

"And if I continue to take liberties with her, what exactly will you do, Derek? Would you really go against your own brother for her sake?"

I knew what he was playing at, testing my loyalties, but I also knew how to play this game. I wanted to believe that we were still gentlemen, after all.

"Give me this courtesy, Lucas. I do not know why, but I'm drawn to her. Consider her your gift to me."

Lucas backed down.

"It's only appropriate I suppose." He managed to say, after a pause. "After all, it was I who found her."

He took one last look at Sofia and removed his arm from her seat. He set his focus straight on me.

"And what exactly do you plan to do with my gift?"

I looked at Sofia and knew from the way she was gazing at me that she too wanted to know the answer to that question.

"I expect her to school me in whatever I missed during my sleep. She's of great value to me in that respect. I also plan to take her to the Crimson Fortress to train her to fight."

"What?!"

It wasn't only Lucas who reacted, but also Vivienne, who had just stepped into the room. Apparently, they felt quite free to enter my quarters whenever they pleased.

Vivienne gave Sofia a wary glance as she took a seat beside me. "Why would you train her to fight? She's a slave, Derek. That makes no sense."

"I intend to keep her for a long time. If she's to stay with me, she needs to know how to defend herself."

"How can you trust her not to use that against you?" Lucas shot at me.

"She won't. I can trust her." I stared at her. "Can't I, Sofia?"

It was more a statement than a question. She gave it a moment's thought and though I knew neither my brother nor sister were convinced she was telling the truth, I fully believed her when she said, "You can."

Chapter 13: Sofia

I will never forget that conversation at Derek's dining table. For one, it was the first conversation I'd ever sat through where the people surrounding me talked about me and my future as if I wasn't present. Only a short while ago, I was really not much of anything other than Benjamin Hudson's shadow. Now I was sitting there, having two vampires argue over which one of them I belonged to.

I wasn't thrilled about "belonging" to anyone, but I'd be a liar if I didn't admit that I was flattered. However, it wasn't the brothers' showdown when it came to who had control over me that made such a distinct impression on me that morning. It was the look in Derek's blazing blue eyes when he asked if he could trust me.

I didn't know why I did it, but then and there, I decided that he could. Still bent on escaping captivity, I wondered to myself how I would pull that off while still maintaining Derek's trust. I realized that if I were to escape, breaking his trust was inevitable. While I was still within the confines of The Shade, however, it was clear that the safest place to be was with Derek.

After my botched escape attempt, I came to realize that I wasn't about to leave The Shade any time soon. If I were to escape, I had to have a strategic plan. Despite my hunger, I was barely able to bite through my breakfast. Lucas' presence was that unnerving. Whenever he was around, I could still remember the way he touched me back at the dungeon. There was no doubt in my mind that without Derek or even Vivienne to reel him in, he would have no reservations about doing whatever he pleased with me. He terrified me, and I could immediately see why Derek was a better man.

Vivienne eyed me warily at that breakfast table and I couldn't help but feel as if she was measuring my worth. She licked her lips before looking at Derek.

"We need to discuss something very important about The Shade, something she can't hear. I don't trust her as much as you seem to."

Derek's eyes lingered on me for a couple of seconds before saying, "You may leave, Sofia."

"And do what?" I couldn't keep myself from asking.

"Entertain yourself... do whatever you wish, but stay in the penthouse. You can have the other girls at your disposal. Find something to do to amuse yourselves."

I raised my eyebrows, surprised that he would trust me after I'd just tried to escape, and surprised at myself for sensing the urge to honor my captor's trust.

"Vivienne said that there are still rooms we can... decorate? May I have one room?"

He looked at me curiously, but most likely saw no harm in my request.

"Of course. I'm sure Vivienne will see to it. Won't you,

Vivienne?"

Vivienne nodded after giving me a quick, irritated look.

"Of course."

I realized how influential Derek was at The Shade. Even Lucas and Vivienne balked at his command. I wondered what made them fear and honor him so much.

I bade my leave, eager to get away from my captors. I weaved my way through the walkways to discover where they kept the other girls. It didn't take long for me to find them, because guards were stationed outside their doors.

"The prince sent me," I told them.

They exchanged glances. One nodded to the other and the guard made his way to Derek – or so I assumed. I had no choice but to wait for him to get back after receiving instructions from Derek himself. I eyed the guard left there with me.

"May I ask you a question?"

He looked surprised that I would even speak with him. "Go ahead."

"Who is Derek Novak exactly? Why is everyone so afraid of him?"

"I would think that after you did the impossible and won his favor so quickly, you'd know more about him than anyone else. You must've pleased him so much that he would actually kill a guard for you."

I found myself uneasy at what he was trying to imply.

"What do you mean *please* him? Do you think…"

"What else would you have done since you got here?"

I could feel the heat rise to my cheeks, flushing as red as the blood running through my veins.

"That's *not*… I would *never!*" I spluttered.

Here I was, a virgin, being rumored to have given the newly

awakened prince a pleasurable night in bed.

He frowned, an amused glint in the corners of his eyes. "You mean you didn't..."

My eyes widened. "No! I'm not that kind of girl..."

"Oh, I'm sure you're not, but can you blame us for thinking that he would be the kind of man who'd be able to make you do things you wouldn't normally do?"

I was rendered speechless. My mouth opened to say something in my defense, but nothing came out. The first thought that came to my mind was, *Derek's not that kind of guy.*

To my relief, the guard seemed over the whole thing. He chuckled, apparently amused by my passionate reaction.

"I'm Samuel," he introduced himself, an easy smile forming on his lips. The blonde man with a lean build and short stubble was only a couple of inches taller than me, though I figured he was somewhere in his twenties when he got turned.

I knew I would be a fool to trust him immediately, but it felt like I'd found a friend in him. I flashed him a small smile.

"Sofia."

"Like I don't know *that*," he winked. "The prince is known to be picky with women. The fact that he's giving you this attention practically makes you a celebrity here."

I wasn't sure how to react to that. I was used to being obscure and invisible. Being told that I was known by everyone was a notion I wasn't used to, but found rather ... flattering.

"To finally answer your question, you're owned by a legend. Derek Novak made The Shade possible. Many vampires survived the hunters because of his leadership. He found this island, built the Crimson Fortress and won Cora, the most powerful witch of their time, over to our side. He is possibly the most powerful and revered vampire on the planet."

I held my breath, taken aback. I knew Derek was important to the coven, but I wasn't expecting him to have all that legendary history backing him up.

"Wow."

"Wow is right," Samuel nodded.

Before I could say anything else, the other guard returned. He shrugged. "The prince instructs us that as long as it doesn't involve allowing them to leave the penthouse, we are to do whatever she says."

Samuel grinned at me. "Looks like we have a new princess." He then pushed the door open to reveal the other girls.

"Sam, dude," the other guard said, "I don't think making friends with the prince's muse is good for your health."

"Relax, Kyle. She's alright."

I gave them a funny look. I was going to like those two. I stepped inside the girls' quarters, not quite knowing what to expect. Four pairs of eyes fell on me as I entered. They all looked relieved to see me. Even though we were still strangers to each other, they acted as though we were long lost friends, as all four girls began throwing their arms around me.

"Are you alright?"

"What did he *do* to you?!"

"He didn't... force you, did he?"

"Do you know what they're going to do to us?"

"Will we ever get home?"

"Have you seen what's outside? Is there any way we can escape?!"

Question after question came at me before I could come up with a single answer. I tried to calm and settle them down so I could speak. I started with:

"I'm fine. He didn't *force* me or hurt me or feed on me. And I don't think he will. I honestly think that while we're here at The Shade, our best chance of survival is to stay in Derek Novak's good graces."

CHAPTER 14: DEREK

Not long after Sofia left us to discuss whatever it was that Vivienne saw as too confidential for her to hear, my siblings took me on a tour of the island, mainly the Crimson Fortress, showing me how they'd fortified it over the past centuries. What used to be merely a wall surrounding the island, was now home to over three hundred vampire guards and scouts who sought refuge at The Shade and swore to defend it.

In a number of strategic areas of the fortress, there were large stone houses with pointed turrets in front of the buildings that lined the wall. I was told that several of the men and women belonging to the Elite trained for battle and were called Knights. The homes were theirs for times when they were called to duty to the wall.

The Elite consisted of the twenty original clans who swore allegiance to our family. They were those who fought and bled with us, tracked down by the hunters until we finally found sanctuary at

The Shade. Everyone else – guards, scouts and the lodgers – came only after the wall was built and Cora's spell was able to provide permanent protection to The Shade.

"Where do most of the human slaves stay?"

"Aside from the beauties that we keep in our homes for our entertainment, all the humans stay at the Black Heights." Lucas' eyes twinkled at the mention of "the beauties". My brother had always had a penchant for beautiful young women.

"The mountains?" I asked.

"We divided the network of caves we found there into the Cells and the slave quarters. Prisoners and newfound human captives – before they are assigned – are sent to the Cells. Humans live in the slave quarters, which they call the Catacombs," Vivienne explained.

"The Catacombs?" I asked curiously.

"I see irony is lost on you." Lucas rolled his eyes. "At The Shade, it is the living who get to reside within the Catacombs."

I eyed the height of the wall protecting us. "Everything seems in order. I don't understand why it was necessary that I wake from my sleep."

"Things won't always be alright, Derek," Vivienne enthused. "The hunters are more powerful than ever. They're technologically advanced and have the support of wealthy and influential people. The Shade remains undiscovered and safe, but other covens aren't. The Shade is no longer a secret in vampire communities and other covens have threatened to attack us or expose us unless we take them in or find them a refuge of their own."

I grimaced. These same covens were the ones that shunned us and left us to die when we needed their help against the hunters. Now they were threatening to spill our blood if we didn't save them?

"What have we been doing about this then?"

"As we've already told you, father is meeting with the heads of other covens. From the last we heard of him, all covens will be dispatching their leaders or at least an ambassador to arrive here so we can talk further about a compromise."

"And I need to be awake for these talks because...?"

"My thoughts exactly," Lucas mumbled.

I gave him a wary glance, wondering how it was possible that he hadn't matured even the slightest after all this time. In his head, we were still obviously competing... for what, I had no idea any more.

"You command respect from all the other covens in a way none of us could, they know what you did. They will listen to you," Vivienne said. "And it's not just that. I really don't think that we can keep The Shade a secret from the hunters for long. Not even with Corrine maintaining Cora's spell. The hunters have been wondering where all these vampires have been disappearing to. And with us needing the humans and having to abduct them just to stay alive... that won't just go away. Investigations are being done by several security agencies about all these missing people. We can't keep this up for long."

I clenched my fists. "What makes you think that I would know how to fix this, Vivienne? I did my part. I brought you to sanctuary just like your prophecy said. Why can't someone else take this on? Why not Father?"

"The prophecy was that your reign alone can provide our kind true sanctuary. The Shade has been *a* sanctuary for a limited number of our kind, but it isn't yet a true sanctuary until we either find all vampires a safe haven and manage a way to survive without the need of humans, or..."

"Or what?" I said, casting a stern look at my sister.

She spoke the blood-curdling words I was expecting. "We have to end the hunters once and for all."

"You're talking about war and bloodshed that we can't even imagine. How long has it even been since The Shade's guards have been in actual battle?"

All I got from my sister was silence.

We continued our trek through the island, leaving the issue hanging in the air. It weighed heavily on me for the rest of the time I spent with them. To say that I wasn't burdened by what I'd been told was a lie. I didn't understand why I had to stand as the leader. I was younger than a lot of the men there.

I was ready to go home and retreat to solitude – not willing to be around the human slaves. Not even Sofia. She was so human – a reminder of what I was and who I was before I became so defined by the creature I'd transformed into.

I was already intent on going back to my quarters when Vivienne held my arm and pulled me toward her. She didn't provide an explanation. She led me through the walkways until we reached a spare room. She pushed the door open and revealed an unconscious woman lying in the center of the bed. "She used to be a hunter – one of the newer, weaker ones. She was brought here by one of the lodgers as a sort of payment for allowing him and his sister to take refuge here at The Shade."

"Why are you telling me this?" I asked, unable to deny that the woman splayed out on the bed in front of me was attractive.

"I thought you might be tired of drinking blood from a glass and would enjoy a fresh meal." Vivienne smiled, looking pleased with herself.

She knew the fact that this one was a hunter made the prospect even more appealing. I licked my lips and stepped forward. Vivienne took that as approval and stepped out of the room.

"Enjoy," she said just before she closed the door, leaving me to do as I pleased with her slave.

There was no hesitation on my part. The darkness within me took over. I was beside the woman, pulling her against me and sinking my teeth into her neck. The taste of hot blood, pumping through her veins by a living beating heart, was invigorating. I drank, determined to bleed her dry. I kept telling myself for all those years that I hated being a vampire, but it was who I was and as I drank from this woman, there was no escaping it.

I sucked the blood out of my young victim and just as I was about to drink the last drop – the one that would cause her heart to stop beating, a moment of clarity came to me. For reasons I could not understand – and I wasn't sure I even wanted to – I realized that the whole time I was holding this beautiful stranger in my arms, feeding on her, it felt like I was betraying Sofia.

Chapter 15: Sofia

It was impossible to know that Derek had already arrived back at the Residences. The girls – Gwen, Ashley, Paige, and Rosa – and I were in the kitchen making what we assumed would be dinner. It was hard to tell considering the lack of sunlight, but we all decided that we were starving.

We were actually having a good time. I'd already told the girls that there was no way of escaping – at least not yet – not until we had a solid plan, so we just went through the day trying to do what Derek had suggested – entertain ourselves. We watched TV, read books, and made plans for what I wanted to do with the extra room Derek allowed me to have. Even the guards, Sam and Kyle, seemed to be enjoying our company. They definitely showed no signs of wanting to suck any of us dry.

So when Derek barged into the penthouse, screaming my name like it was bloody murder, I had no idea what I'd done wrong or why he seemed so angry with me. I felt nothing but sheer terror as I approached him as quickly as my legs could carry me.

He was standing in the middle of the living room, muscles tensed, blood dripping from the corners of his lips, looking more menacing than I'd ever seen him before. His muscular physique bulged with his every breath as he took steady strides toward me.

"What happened?" I managed to squeak out.

In response, he grabbed my shoulders and lifted me off the ground. I inwardly groaned, pretty sure that my back was once again about to hit a wall or some other surface hard enough to cause my body damage. Instead, I found myself being pushed onto a couch while he paced the floor in front of me, exuding intensity I'd never seen in anyone. I gripped the arm rests of the couch – a way of bracing myself for whatever outburst this vampire was about to throw my way.

Watching Derek act like a bull seeing red, I wondered if all vampires were like him. Brooding and intense and incapable of laughter or even the slightest hint of mirth … I recalled Sam and Kyle and how they seemed to be in such a light and casual mood when dealing with us girls that afternoon. I wondered how they could be relaxed while the Novaks were so intense and uptight.

Derek stopped pacing and stood right in front of me. He then sat over the edge of the coffee table and rested his elbows on his knees, his hands clasped together and eyes downcast, before he finally spoke his mind.

"What you told me that night… at the Sanctuary, when you first saw me… why did you say it?"

I struggled to recall what I told him. His presence was so overpowering, so consuming, it felt like he was filling up the entire room.

"I don't remember…"

"I was about to feed on you." He said, impatiently. "I told you that I couldn't help myself. You said…"

"…that I know an excuse when I hear one and that you shouldn't make yourself out to be the victim."

"Am I a victim?"

I stared at him for a couple of seconds, wondering if he realized how insane that question sounded coming from his mouth. He wasn't the one who was captured against his own will and imprisoned - in an admittedly breathtaking and lavish penthouse, but imprisoned nonetheless. He was lord of the vampires, feared, revered and admired. How on earth could he be a victim?

I studied his appearance, wondering what was going through his mind. Before I could even think it through I reached out and wiped the blood off his mouth with a tissue.

"You fed on someone."

It was almost as if he stopped breathing and his fists clenched again.

"She wasn't much older than you. Eighteen or nineteen. She was a hunter. She was the enemy. I found pleasure sucking out every drop of her blood." He raised his blue eyes to meet mine and the faintest smirk formed on his lips. "I enjoyed it the same way I would've enjoyed you."

My stomach writhed. I was confused by what he was attempting to say. "Why are you telling me this, Derek?"

A painful expression twisted his handsome features as he began to fidget with his fingers. He shook his head slowly before responding, "Because I don't want to enjoy it. I actually miss being the victim, but that night … you saw me as someone playing the part of a victim. Why?"

I gave it some thought. *Why did I say that?* At the time, all I wanted was for him to spare my life, but I could've said so many things. Why that? I dared place my hand over his before answering.

"Because I don't believe that you are a slave to what you've become. I don't believe that you *simply can't.*"

He looked at me with so much intensity, I began to wonder if I'd said something wrong, so I was relieved when his expression finally relaxed and he lifted a hand to brush a stray strand of hair away from my face.

"You are a marvel."

I had to smile at this ridiculous statement.

"Not compared to you." I teased.

"What do you mean?" He seemed taken aback.

"The guards told us that you're a legend, savior of the vampires. It all sounded rather impressive."

He looked away, as if he was disturbed by my words. After all he'd accomplished, I would have expected him to be proud, to gloat over it, to puff out his chest and have that look on his face letting everyone know that it was indeed him who *did that.* It's definitely how Ben would've reacted.

Not Derek.

"Savior of the vampires…" he scoffed. "I'm supposed to rule over our kind. They say my reign will bring the vampires true sanctuary. I'm not sure we even deserve to be saved. After everything we've done … After everything we're doing…" He gave me a long, meaningful gaze and pulled his hand away from my grasp. "Look at what we're doing to you."

I didn't know how to respond. I missed Ben so much. There hadn't been a waking moment since my arrival when he wasn't at the back of my mind, when I wasn't wondering what he was thinking about or how he was dealing with my disappearance. I wondered how many of the humans they brought here were separated from loved ones. To my relief, Derek didn't seem to be interested in a response.

"My father was a farmer," he began. "That's what we did before we became … *this*. We farmed wheat and grew vegetables. It was a humble existence, but we were happy. Then one night, my father and Lucas were out in the city to trade our goods. Vivienne and I went out for wood. When we returned, our mother was dead, her blood sucked dry."

I swallowed hard as I listened.

"Vivienne swore it was a wild beast. They ridiculed me but I knew it was a vampire. I was just thirteen at the time, but I was so sure that a vampire murdered my mother, I found a way to join the hunters. For five years, I was one of them and I killed many, many vampires. So imagine my surprise when, on my eighteenth birthday, my father came home and he was a vampire. I should've killed him. I really should've, but I couldn't. He was still my father. He turned Lucas, Vivienne and me that night. I became the very creature that I hunted, the creature that I hated."

"If you hate vampires so much, why fight to save them? Why establish The Shade?"

"It was never about saving vampires. The next hundred years after I was turned were all about saving my family. It just so happened that I couldn't save them without also saving the others who helped us survive. I never thought that The Shade would become what it is now."

I couldn't even begin to imagine what those years were like for him, how tormented he must have felt, but if he wanted me to acknowledge that he was a victim to his own existence, I wasn't about to give him that. He was too strong, too powerful, and too influential to play the part of a victim.

"I'm sorry for what you had to go through, and I'm...honored that you would tell me these things, but you're strong and you're a leader – whether you like it or not. If anything, you seem to be the only one here who has the power to change things ... for the better."

"I don't know how to do that."

"Well, who said you have to figure it all out tonight?"

I don't know what possessed me to do it, but I grabbed his hand and nudged him toward the larger couch, enjoying the curiosity in his eyes as I sat next to him. I sighed before pulling his arm around my shoulder and snuggling against his chest.

"We've already had too much drama for one night, don't you think?"

"I suppose so." His tone seemed lighter, more relaxed as he ran his fingers over my bare shoulder. "Now that I've embarrassingly spilled my guts to you, perhaps it's time you told me more about yourself."

I groaned. "And delve into *my* drama? I don't think so. Let's spend tonight introducing you to today's version of entertainment."

I reached for the remote control and switched on the flat-screen TV. I smiled at the fascination that sparked in his eyes.

"What on bloody earth is that?" he asked.

"A magic mirror," I teased, before doing my best to explain to him what exactly a television set was. I asked if he wanted to watch a movie, recalling the extensive DVD collection we'd found earlier that night. I told him to pick a movie and he returned with two interesting choices: *Chicago* and *the Godfather*. It was almost a reflection of the kind of person that he was – a musician and a killer whose loyalty to family stood above all else – either way, tormented, with darkness constantly looming over him.

Since I wasn't up for watching either movie, I smiled, remembering his request and how Vivienne managed to have her minions see that it was done immediately.

"I have a better idea."

I was amused by the questioning look he gave me as I stood up, laid the DVDs he chose on the center table, grabbed his hand and pulled him toward the music room. The sheer delight in his eyes when he saw the room was almost endearing – like he was a young boy being shown a room full of his favorite toys.

"Vivienne did it so quickly…"

"Your sister really loves you…" There was bitterness in the way I said the words, jealous that he had family who worshiped the ground he walked on, while all I had was a family that had abandoned me and left me to another's care.

He sat in front of the black grand piano and tapped on the space next to him. "Sit."

I noted how he never said *please* to me. With him, there were never requests, just commands. I rolled my eyes, still not used to being told what to do. The Hudsons never really paid much attention to what I did or didn't do as long as I didn't get myself or their kids into trouble. Ben wasn't very authoritative either. This was something about Derek I thought I'd never get used to, but still, I found myself sitting next to him as he played an enthralling tune that simply took my breath away.

In the middle of his performance, it dawned on me that this was exactly the effect Derek Novak had on me: he always managed to – in one way or another – take my breath away.

Chapter 16: Derek

She looked so peaceful, so serene, so innocent, as I carried her to her bedroom and laid her on the bed. No other woman – and believe me when I say that I've been with many – had the same effect that Sofia Claremont had on me. She was fragile and vulnerable, yet strong and resilient at the same time. She'd only recently entered my life, yet it felt like I'd known her for ages.

It was grateful for the way she listened to me and tried to ease my mind after my tempestuous outburst. But at the same time, I was frustrated. Inside the music room, she listened to me give in to my passion for music. She listened until exhaustion and sleep stole her attention away from me. Lying on the cushioned wooden bench inside the music room, she was a feast to behold, with her dress hiking up those long, milky white legs of hers, her locks of dark auburn hair flowing down the edge of the bench, and her pink lips slightly parting as she breathed. My stomach clenched just looking at her, wondering why she would allow herself to be so vulnerable around a creature like me – one who could lose control at any moment and completely ruin her.

But somehow, deep inside, I knew... I knew that I could never harm her in that way, simply because I would never be able to forgive myself for it. I may not have enough self-control to keep myself from feeding on others, but with Sofia, I couldn't afford to lose control. She had become my one remaining link to humanity and it was clear to me that her ruin would be my ruin.

I carefully picked her up in my arms, fully aware of how much of the skin on her neck and shoulders was exposed to me and how much her smell was luring me in. However, this time it was easier for me to hold myself back. She had managed to make herself too precious to me.

I left her on the round bed covered with pink linens and white furs. There was a smile on my face as I walked out of her room. With Sofia, it felt like I'd finally found my compass. I knew that as long as I had her, I had someone to keep me grounded, someone to direct my way. If only for Sofia, I had a reason to stay awake.

Having absolutely no desire – or need – to lose myself in sleep, I returned to the living room and figured out how to view the "movies" she'd introduced to me. I was amazed by the contraptions society had managed to create over the years. I never would've dreamed them possible in my day.

Hours passed as I viewed one movie after another, moved by the stories and lives portrayed. I had to remind myself several times what Sofia had told me – it wasn't real, just actors playing a part – like in the theaters of my time.

I was in a good mood when morning came and was eager to check on Sofia. So, when I knocked on her door, I wasn't expecting to be met with silence. I knocked again. Nothing. My heart sank as I assumed the worst. I was certain that despite my warning, she'd once again attempted to escape. I swung the door open and looked around the room. The smell of blood immediately invaded my senses and I was stunned to find that my first instinct wasn't hunger but instead, an overwhelming urge to make sure Sofia was unharmed.

An emotion I wasn't quite accustomed to engulfed me when I saw her. It was a strange mixture of alarm, concern and protectiveness. She was sitting in one corner of the room, trembling as she held her legs tightly against her chest. Her green eyes betrayed complete and utter terror.

I knew something was horribly wrong, but I couldn't even begin to imagine what could've happened to cause such a reaction from her.

"Sofia?" I choked.

I knelt in front of her and tried to brush her hair away from her face. She flinched at my touch – a stark contrast to how comfortable and secure she'd felt with me the night before when she spontaneously snuggled against me on the couch and while I was playing the piano.

A sick feeling churned in the pit of my stomach as one possibility after another flooded through my mind.

"What happened, Sofia?!" I urged.

I couldn't understand what was causing her to behave like this. Her lips were trembling so profusely, I was certain that I wouldn't understand anything that came out of her mouth even if she chose to answer my question. That's when I noticed something she was clutching with her shaking right fist. I didn't want to invade her space at a time like this but I was desperate to find out what was going on. Ignoring the way she flinched, I pried her hands open.

It was a lock of light blonde hair. I frowned in confusion. Suddenly one of the guards came running through the open door.

"Your highness?" he spoke up.

"What?" I asked, not bothering to look at him.

"One of your girls - Gwen. She's … she's missing!"

My jaw tightened as I realized what had likely happened. I made my way toward Sofia's bathroom, noticing that the door had been left ajar. I pushed it open.

Rage I hadn't felt for centuries began to consume me. In a bloody pool of water, Gwen's lifeless body lay in the bath tub. On her wrists were bite marks. Someone had bled her dry.

It was a deliberate affront to me and a blatant threat toward Sofia. The guard, who was right behind me, gasped at the sight.

"You were supposed to be keeping watch of the girls! How did this happen?!" I growled, desperately trying to reel in my temper.

"Sir, I … I don't know… I…"

I moved fast and pinned him to the wall. I looked into his eyes and saw an air of dignity there. Unlike the guard, Husky, I'd killed not long ago, this one wasn't about to beg for his life. He knew he was innocent and I knew it too.

I backed down and loosened my grip on him.

"Whoever did this, dies. Find out who has insulted me in this way."

I walked toward Sofia and, ignoring her struggles to push me away, I gathered her in my arms and carried her out of the room. I didn't know where to take her but I was damned certain that I couldn't just leave her there. Once she realized that I wasn't about to let her go, she eased into my arms and buried her face against my chest before letting go of the emotions she had pent up inside. Tears began to stream down her lovely face and I wanted nothing more than to rip the beating heart out of the person who put her through this.

However, there was a truth I kept denying to myself: there was only one person at The Shade who would dare stand up to me by pulling a stunt like this. *My own brother, Lucas.*

Chapter 17: Sofia

Everything happened in a blur. I was aware of it all, and yet, I wasn't. It was almost like everything was happening to another person, and yet it was me. I felt Derek's strong arms grab hold of me. I heard his conversation with Vivienne before they both decided to take me to see Corrine, the witch at the Sanctuary. I saw the agitation in Derek's face, the intoxicating scent of his natural musk filling my nostrils as I snuggled against him.

I was conscious of it all, and yet, at the same time, I was stuck in a memory, still reliving every sickening sensation it induced.

I was lured to sleep by an enchanting melody and awakened from it by a horrific nightmare.

His hand was clamped over my mouth and his full weight was rested on top of me, constricting my breathing. I felt his free hand hike up my thigh and when I flinched, he chuckled vehemently, amused by my weakness.

"I will have you someday, Sofia," he whispered against my ear. "Oh, you will bring me so much pleasure ... and once I'm done with you, I will have a taste of your sweet, sweet blood."

His hand hiked up my waist and slipped beneath my back. Blinding pain unlike anything I'd ever experienced before assaulted me when his claws came out. My screams were muffled by his palm over my mouth as he scratched through my flesh with his nails. My back was on fire. Desperate tears began to stream down my face as the searing agony ripped me apart.

His mouth pressed against my chest, neck, jaw and cheek. Each blood-curdling word hissed from his lips, dripping with spite and the intent to make me feel he had complete power over me.

"But don't worry, my fragile little twig. I've had my fill for the night. I just wanted to warn you what's ahead of you. You know, remind you who found you ... and who *really* owns you."

Still keeping his hand over my mouth, Lucas lifted himself up on the bed, so that he was kneeling over me, straddling my hips as he looked down at me, a manic smile on his face.

"Don't get too comfortable with my brother, Sofia, because no matter what he may think, you're mine. And should you get any bright ideas about telling Derek about this little rendezvous of ours, consider this a stern warning."

He used his free hand to retrieve something from his jacket pocket. It was a lock of blonde hair. My eyes grew wide with horror imagining what the object implied. He began tracing the ends of the strands of hair over my jaw line.

"I have a gift waiting for you in the bathroom. Before you scream for help, I suggest you check it out ... unless, of course, you want more of my gifts waiting for you..."

With that, he left, leaving the lock of hair behind. Trembling, I grabbed the item and got off the bed. I slowly walked toward the bathroom, dreading to find out what "gift" he could possibly think of giving me. When I opened the bathroom door and found Gwen's limp body there, the sensations and emotions that rushed through me were more than I could handle. My throat felt so dry, I couldn't even scream. I just retreated to a corner, terrified, realizing that no matter how beautiful The Shade was on the outside, it was only a mask to hide its darkness. I'd fooled myself into believing that I was safe, but that was the biggest lie I'd told myself in years.

Chapter 18: Derek

"She's wounded," was the first thing Corrine said when I barged through the doors of the Sanctuary, Sofia still sobbing in my arms.

I wondered what she was talking about as I followed Corrine to one of the Sanctuary's chambers. I walked toward the bed in the middle of the room and laid Sofia there. My stomach turned when I saw how bloody one of my hands was. Her blood. My craving for her should've consumed me – it was in my nature to want to taste her – but my desire to make things right with her overpowered every other lustful craving.

"What happened to her?" Corrine asked.

I ignored the witch and flipped Sofia's motionless body over so that she was lying face down on the bed. She made no attempts to stop me when I began ripping the back of her dress open. The sight of her back was revolting. Claws had run the length of her back, etching deep cuts in her flesh. I wondered to myself how someone as fragile as her could sustain such wounds without passing out.

"Who did this to you, Sofia? *Who* killed Gwen?!"

She didn't respond. She just buried her face in the pillow, sobbing frantically. I drew the dagger out of my sleeve and without a moment's hesitation made a deep, long cut in my palm. I grabbed Sofia's arm and with my agitation and the sense of urgency I felt, yanked her to an upright, sitting position. She gasped in pain at the sudden motion.

"Derek…" Vivienne spoke from behind me. "She's already in enough pain."

I wasn't even aware that my sister had followed us all the way there.

"There's no time. She needs to heal fast. We don't know how much blood she's already lost."

I was inwardly chastising myself for not having noticed her wounds while still back in the bedroom. I pressed my palm over Sofia's mouth, my other hand positioned at the back of her neck.

"Drink," I ordered.

I was relieved that she didn't put up a fight and relented. Perhaps she just wanted the pain to stop and knew well enough that my blood in her system would exceedingly speed up the healing process. I didn't care. As long as I felt her soft mouth sucking on the blood from my palm, I was satisfied. It did little to ease the fury I felt inside, but it did wonders for the worry I felt over her predicament.

Relief washed over me when the cuts on her back began to heal. She must've felt it, because she stopped drinking from my palm. I was so distraught over what happened to her under my watch that I wanted her to keep drinking as if my blood could fix *everything* for her. The gash on my palm closed however, and I watched her wipe the blood from her face with her arm. I wanted to see the light in her eyes flicker back on, any indication that the fire within her hadn't died out, but her blank stare told me otherwise as she listlessly laid her head back on the pillow.

"What's going on? What did you do to her?" Corrine eyed me suspiciously, making it clear that she didn't trust me the way her ancestor, Cora, did.

"I didn't do *anything* to her," I replied indignantly. "I found her this way when I checked on her this morning."

"One of the other girls in his harem was found murdered – bled dry – inside her bathroom," Vivienne added.

Corrine kept up her suspicious perusal of me. "And *you* didn't do this?"

I glared at her, trying to maintain my patience. "Did you not hear me the first time, witch?"

"Can you blame me for thinking you had something to do with this? You took one look at her when you woke up and threw her up a pillar, more than ready to devour her. Who knows what sick things you have in mind to do to her…"

"Corrine, he didn't do this," Vivienne spoke up knowing that if she didn't, I might not be able to keep myself from maiming the witch for her insolence.

"Well then, who did?" Corrine raised an eyebrow. "You creatures sicken me."

She wrinkled her nose and looked at Vivienne and myself as if we were the most despicable things she'd ever laid eyes on. I wasn't so sure she was wrong, but the witch's hypocrisy was getting on my nerves.

"If you hate us so much, why do you serve us? Why help protect us?"

"Your kind took me captive much like you did this girl. I had no choice in the matter."

This was news to me. "Is this true, Vivienne?"

"We needed a witch to keep the spell going…" Vivienne tried to explain.

I was perhaps losing half my mind because I looked at Corrine and in all seriousness, I said, "You're free to go any time you please, witch. No one will stop you. You have my word."

"Derek…" Vivienne gasped. "We can't…"

"Be quiet, Vivienne." I lifted a hand to silence my sister. I stared at the shocked expression on Corrine's face. "You're no longer a prisoner of The Shade, Corrine. You may leave today if you wish. I'll even see you to the port myself."

I was calling her bluff. She was Cora's descendant and if she was anything like her ancestor, no one would have been able to keep her in one place against her will. She was here for a reason and it certainly wasn't because we kept her locked up.

Corrine eyed me for a couple of seconds, her lips sealed tight. Then, a small sideward smile formed on her face.

"I see now what Cora saw in you."

Vivienne stepped forward, looking utterly confused.

"Corrine … you mean, you're not leaving? You've been harping on about being held against your will since you got here."

"You really are quite a lovely thing, aren't you, Vivienne? I've inherited hundreds of years' worth of power and knowledge from Cora down to every descendant she had. Do you really think you can hold me captive with four walls or a cage?" Corrine then looked back at Sofia. She sighed heavily. "Now let's get back to the matter at hand. If I'm to find out what really happened, I can't have either of you lurking around, threatening her."

"I would *never* threaten her," I spat out.

"Don't kid yourself, Derek," Corrine smirked. "Your presence alone is a threat to her. Now, go on … *shoo*. Leave now."

I cast a lingering glance at Sofia, feeling like I was being ripped apart from the inside. I gave the arrogant young witch a heartfelt plea. "Do everything you can to make things right for her… just … fix her."

There was a spark of confusion in Corrine's large brown eyes. Perhaps she was wondering why I cared so much, but she didn't address the matter and instead, simply herded Vivienne and myself out of the room.

"You can see yourselves out. I will have a guard alert you once she is ready to return to the Pavilion."

I stood outside as Corrine slammed the door in our faces. I didn't budge from my spot, determined to stay there and wait until Sofia was cured.

Vivienne grabbed my hand and squeezed.

"Sofia's going to be fine. Corrine was in her senior year of psychology when we dragged her down here. She'll know how to help Sofia."

"I'm not leaving until I know Sofia is cured." I announced.

My sister knew me well enough to know that once I put my mind to something, I was as stubborn as a mule. She nodded, realizing that nothing she could say would convince me to leave that place.

"If you need me, I'll be at the Pavilion seeing to the investigations. We'll find out who did this, Derek."

I crossed my arms over my chest. I felt guilt and shame come over me as Vivienne left me there to brood alone. I couldn't think of anyone who could be capable of doing this to Sofia other than Lucas. But I had no proof and even if I did, I wasn't sure that I could do anything about it. Lucas was my brother and no matter how important Sofia had become to me, blood runs thicker than water.

Chapter 19: Sofia

Corrine took her time with me. She tried to make me comfortable, giving me a drink of water, which I truly appreciated, considering how the taste of Derek's blood was still fresh in my mouth. She took great care in making sure that I wanted to do what she was asking me to do – never pushing or ordering or commanding, which is exactly what Derek would've done had I been left under his care.

She gave me a fresh set of clothes to wear. I was so relieved to see that she handed me skinny jeans and an adorable-looking white baby doll blouse. It was nice to see something I would wear in normal life, instead of the dresses and skirts afforded to me at the Pavilion. They were pretty and feminine, but it felt like the sole reason I had to wear them was so that the vampires could have easy access to my body – that's certainly what Lucas got. I put on the jeans knowing how irrational my line of thinking was. It's not like I would've worn jeans to sleep in the first place. Still, the snug fit of the denim on my legs

102

provided me a thread of comfort. *At least I won't have to feel Lucas'*
hands on my legs. I shuddered, recalling the way he touched me. I
knew that it wasn't going to be the last time he would do it. What
terrified me most was how helpless I felt at the time. I never wanted
to feel that way again.

"Would you like to talk about what happened?" Corrine asked.

I sat over the edge of her bed as she pulled an ottoman in front of
me so she could sit right across me. From her bedside table, she
pointed to a bowl of fruit.

"If you're hungry…" she offered.

I shook my head. "No, thank you."

I truly appreciated the way she was treating me. It was like she was
the caring older sister I never had.

"What happened, Sofia? I promise that whatever you say, it won't
leak out of this room unless you want it to."

"I don't remember," I lied. I remembered every single detail. "I
woke up and I had the cuts on my back and the lock of Gwen's hair
in my hand. I walked to the bathroom and…" I choked, recalling
Gwen's fate. "She didn't deserve to die."

I knew I had to protect the other girls from what happened to
Gwen. Lucas' threat was still ringing in my ear. I had no doubt in my
mind that he wouldn't hesitate to destroy me and the girls the first
chance he got.

"You're right. She didn't." Corrine nodded. Her brown eyes bore
into mine. "Sofia, I can't help you unless you're honest with me. Was
it Derek who did this to you?"

"He already told you that he didn't."

"Yes, but I want to hear it from you."

I was surprised by the protectiveness I felt toward Derek. I almost
felt insulted that anyone would imply that he could do something

like this.

"If Derek did this, then there wouldn't be any fuss, would there? We're his slaves after all. Is he not allowed to do as he pleases with us? The only reason that this is such a big deal is because someone else most likely did it and it's a huge insult to Derek."

Corrine smiled, almost as if she were proud that I came up with that answer myself. It felt as if she was playing mind games with me.

"The prince seems to care a lot about you. He seemed pretty distraught to see you in this state."

I remained silent. I felt so hurt and abused. I was scared of what was to come. I wanted to believe so badly that Derek cared enough about me to choose me over his brother, but if he had endured being a creature he hated for hundreds of years just to save his family, what could make me think that he would choose me over Lucas?

Corrine most likely saw that she wasn't going to get anywhere with her line of questioning, so she tried a different approach.

"Is it alright if you tell me what your time at The Shade has been like for you? I'm rather curious to know."

That I saw no harm in doing and I found myself opening up to her. I spilled out every sensation still fresh in my memory, every fear, every apprehension, and even stolen moments of delight and wonder. I told her how much I missed my best friend and how worried I was about him. I didn't know why I did it. Perhaps it was just the need for a friend, an ally. The only thing I kept from her was what Lucas did to me and the threat he gave me should I tell a soul about it.

I did, however, make myself a promise as I was having that conversation with Corrine. I promised myself that Lucas wasn't going to get away with what he did to Gwen. *Sooner or later, he will pay.*

Chapter 20: Derek

I rose to my feet the moment the door swung open. I breathed out a sigh of relief when Sofia's lovely form stepped out of the room, a tentative smile spreading across her lips at the sight of me. If only out of sheer relief, I wanted to pull her into my arms and kiss her right then and there, but I fought the urge to do it in fear of scaring her. So I held back and allowed her to set the pace. I doubt she was aware of the effect she had on me when she walked toward me, grabbed my hand; her thin, dainty fingers intertwining with mine before she lifted my hand and placed a soft kiss over the back of it.

I didn't fully understand why she did it, but I took it as assurance that she still felt safe around me, that she was choosing to trust me. I was both humbled and pressured by the gesture. I stared at her for a moment. I let my eyes feast on the delicateness of her facial features, adoring every bit of her as I squeezed her hands, treasuring the warmth she exuded.

My perusal of my beautiful captive was interrupted when Corrine cleared her throat.

"May I speak with you in private … Prince?" She tacked on the title as if it were a taunt.

I grimaced, hating that I had to let go of Sofia's hand, but was overcome with curiosity over what the witch would have to say. I motioned to a guard to stand near Sofia and then faced her.

"You're going to be alright?" I asked in a choked whisper.

Sofia nodded. "Go."

I entered Corrine's chambers and she closed the door behind us.

"I must admit I didn't see what you saw in her at first. I couldn't understand what was so special about Sofia Claremont to make you so taken by her, but I get it now."

I leaned forward, interested in what she had to say.

"I'm not certain, but I believe she has a condition that I would like to look into further. I'd like to have her come to me daily … It won't take long. All I require is an hour or two each day."

I didn't fully trust the witch, but was intrigued by her sudden interest in Sofia.

"What condition?"

"It's nothing to be concerned about. It's nothing deadly. If I'm right about her, however, then you've found yourself quite a catch in the young girl. There aren't many like her."

She was telling me what I already knew. I doubted that there was anyone quite like Sofia. Much as I wanted to hear more about this "condition" Sofia supposedly had, I was more concerned by the immediate matter at hand.

"Did she tell you who did it?"

"She claims not to remember."

"Do you believe her?"

Corrine shook her head. "No. She's too smart, too aware, not to remember. She's protecting something… someone."

"Why would she protect whoever did this?"

"Maybe it's not her assailant that she's protecting." Corrine shrugged and stood up straight, giving me an expression that meant business. "I suggest that you make sure she's protected at all times. I also suggest that you not bombard her with questions about what happened. If she's ready to tell you, I'm sure she will. Stop forcing her to do things just because you're the ruler of this bloody Kingdom and your word is law. Respect her by making her feel like she has a choice!"

I wanted to defend myself, tell Corrine that I never forced Sofia to do anything against her will, but I knew what Corrine was trying to say. I wasn't exactly doling out *pleases* and *thank-yous* Sofia's way either. I spoke to her in orders and commands, taking advantage of her obvious fear of me to make her cooperate. I kept convincing myself that I saw humans as equal, if not superior, to vampires, yet I didn't exactly treat Sofia as an equal. I treated her just like everyone else at The Shade did – a captive, a slave.

I gave Corrine a long look before nodding. "Thank you. She'll be back tomorrow…" I headed for the door and paused just before twisting the knob. "That is, if she wants to."

The witch smiled – a show of approval perhaps.

"Have a good day, Derek."

Chapter 21: Sofia

The moment our eyes met, he looked away, almost as if he were embarrassed about something. It was actually... *cute* – a word I never thought I'd use to describe Derek Novak. As we walked back to the Pavilion, he remained silent, deep in thought, never even looking my way.

"You said that you wanted to teach me how to defend myself..." I eventually said, breaking the silence, detesting the wall that seemed to be building up between us.

"Yes," he nodded. He then paused as if to catch himself. "But if you don't want to..."

I frowned. *Since when does he care what I want?*

"I want to."

The heaviness in our conversation was weighing on me. I wanted to go back to how comfortable and casual our interactions were before things took a turn for the worse. *Before Lucas happened.* I was still shaken, still afraid of what Lucas was capable of, but dwelling on woes really wasn't one of my strong suits. It was one of Ben's major influences on me. He never allowed me to dwell on self-pity. So I slipped my hands into Derek's, hoping to let him know that what happened hadn't changed my view of him.

"I'd like it if you let the other girls join in too," I suggested, squeezing his hand.

The gesture seemed to lighten his mood a bit. His shoulders relaxed and his eyes softened.

"Of course." He said.

He then stopped walking and held both my hands closer to him. He heaved a sigh and weighed every word carefully as he spoke.

"I'm thinking that you should start sleeping in my chambers from now on."

I was taken aback. Then a teasing smile crept over my lips.

"Don't you think we're moving a little too fast?"

I joked, squinting an eye at him. I was making fun of his proposal, but the truth was that I had quite a handful of reservations about being in the same bedroom – much more the same bed - with a blood-sucking vampire.

He gave me a funny look, perhaps wondering if he should take me seriously or not.

"I mean it, Sofia. I understand you have reservations, but I promise I won't try anything with you. I just want to make sure you're safe."

I made a conscious effort to keep my jaw from dropping. *Was he actually asking for my consent? He wasn't just ordering me to sleep in his bed? Have we gone past the "no questions asked because his oh-so-royal word was the be-all and end-all of my entire existence"?* I gave it some thought. The idea of returning to my bedroom at the penthouse sickened me. I wasn't sure if I trusted Derek enough to keep his word and not actually try to jump on me, but then the alternative of being alone in a room, and the chance of once again having Lucas climb into my bed in the middle of the night was a far less attractive option.

I nodded and looked up into those bright blue eyes of his.

"I can trust you, can't I, Derek?"

The expression on his face and the way he responded was enough to tell me that he wasn't taking the situation lightly.

He nodded. "Yes, Sofia. You can."

In the days that followed, he proved his words true. Derek never did anything or even said anything to violate my trust. It seemed he took extra care in making sure that I wanted to do what he was asking me to do, and that really was the major difference. He actually began to *ask*. It seemed so unlike him at first … almost unnatural, but as time passed, we became a lot more used to having each other around. Or at least I did.

Days – or in The Shade's case - nights fell into routine. We started off with breakfast before he brought the girls and me to the Crimson Fortress to train using weapons of defense against vampires. Much to his siblings' horror, he actually gave us each wooden stakes of our own. He, however, warned us sternly that those were for self-defense and nothing else. Should we use them for any other purpose, he made it clear that he wouldn't hesitate to kill us himself. It was a reminder that the fierce and menacing part of him was still in there – no matter how caring and gentle he could be around me.

After training sessions, he would have Sam and Kyle bring the girls back to the penthouse to prepare lunch while he brought me to Corrine. I had no idea what he did while I spent a full two hours with Corrine, but it didn't bother me all that much. I began to treasure times I spent with the witch. She was definitely far better than the other psychologists I'd been forced to meet with. It didn't take long for her to have a diagnosis of what my mental condition was.

"You don't have any of the disorders those doctors diagnosed you with, Sofia," she explained. "What you have is often confused with other disorders, because it's hard to detect, but I honestly think that you have "Low Latent Inhibition", also known as LLI. Latent inhibition is what allows people to shut down other things so that they can focus on selected things. It's what allows us to not have to deal with all this external and internal stimuli at the same time. After all, the brain can only take so much. You, however, don't have a lot of latent inhibition. That's why you're constantly fully aware of everything going on around you. You can't just shut down and focus on one thing. It can get overwhelming, because you're always open to new stimuli." She paused. "I think it's what your mother had. She wasn't able to handle it … hence, what happened to her…"

I bit my lip. "Does that mean I could end up like her?"

"Most people who have LLI do end up going crazy, Sofia … *unless* they have a high enough IQ to handle it. You're one of those lucky few. Most people who are able to handle LLI have high levels of empathy and are often very perceptive of others. They're creative geniuses."

At that, I scoffed. I doubted I was much of a creative genius. Yet, a lot of what Corrine said about LLI made sense to me. It was perhaps the reason why I was so attuned to all my senses. I'd just assumed that it was normal for everyone to be that way. Maybe I was wrong.

After sessions with Corrine, I spent the rest of the day with Ashley, Paige, and Rosa. We were often watched by several alternating guards assigned to us, but we decided that we liked Sam and Kyle best. Those afternoons were mostly spent with them helping me finish my project in that extra room Derek had given me in the penthouse. We still talked about escaping, but we had no clue how to pull it off. It almost always ended up being a complete downer, so we eventually avoided talking about it. They asked me a lot about that night with Lucas and what happened. I tried to avoid answering them as best I could. I didn't want to scare them.

I managed to convince Derek to allow us to hold a memorial service in honor of Gwen and he eventually allowed it. It was The Shade's first ever memorial held in honor of a human.

I spent most dinnertimes alone with Derek. Sometimes, he talked to me about what happened throughout his day after he left me with Corrine. Most of the time, he just listened. He kept me up to date on investigations regarding my attack and Gwen's murder. I believed that he suspected Lucas; he just couldn't admit it to himself. It only served to strengthen my resolve not to test his loyalties by telling him.

Over the course of several days, I was also finally able to teach him how to use his cell phone. He gave me one of my own and the first thing I tried to do was call Ben. Apparently, whatever was keeping The Shade secret also blocked any calls and messages from leaving the island. Whoever Cora was, I both admired and loathed her for making The Shade so secure.

If not for Lucas, I could honestly say that I was beginning to enjoy living at The Shade. It was harder for him to get to me, with all the security measures Derek had now built up around me at night, but there were still moments when he caught me alone and off guard. Lucas never failed to remind me that a time would come when I'd be his. I never did have an encounter with him that didn't leave me feeling shaken and violated. I hated Lucas with every fiber of my being. It seemed he sensed that and this knowledge only made the whole thing more amusing to him.

Ultimately, it was Derek who made life at The Shade worth living. I began to treasure the nights I sat with him. Most of the time was spent on me trying to introduce a new piece of technology to him, one at a time. Introducing him to the camera was fun. We spent the night snapping pictures of each other and goofing around. It was one of the first times I could remember hearing him laugh freely.

Life at The Shade almost took on a lethargic pace and the life I had before being kidnapped there began to feel like a completely different lifetime. I worried about the girls and how they were coping but they seemed to have accepted that this was their life for now. Occasionally, we were allowed to leave the penthouse to see other parts of The Shade, where we witnessed how other vampires treated their human slaves. It became all the more evident that being under Derek's care was to our advantage.

There were still nights when Derek would come back home after feeding on another gift from Vivienne or from some other vampire paying him homage. I tried not to talk about it. I figured the less I knew, the better – for both him and me.

The time came when we finally finished what I christened the "Sun Room". It took longer than I'd expected, but I was more than excited to show it to Derek.

I could never forget the look on his face when I pulled him into the room and flicked the lights on.

"You told me you haven't seen sunlight in five hundred years," I explained. "Based on the look in your eyes, I could tell you missed it."

"So you did this?" He looked around the room, a mural of a beautiful sandy beach painted on one wall, large mirrors on the other walls to make the room brighter. At the center of the ceiling was a sun roof, composed of LED lights fixed over a glass window, creating the illusion of sunlight streaming through the room.

We chose outdoor furniture that would create the feel of being out in the open.

I smiled at Derek. "It wasn't just me. Vivienne was more than happy to get us everything we needed. The girls and Sam and Kyle helped too. I guess it's not just you who misses sunlight, so thanks for giving me the idea."

To my surprise, he gently slid his arms around my waist and pulled me against him. He took my arms and laid them over his shoulders and around his neck. He then held me and led me to a slow dance.

"There's no music," I reminded him in a whisper.

He grinned. "In my head, Sofia, there's *always* music."

I found the thought funny. "That must be interesting. It's like you always come with your own background music."

He nodded, smiling down at me. "Exactly."

He then pulled me closer and placed a soft kiss over my forehead. His kiss then fell on my cheek, then to the corner of my lips. I knew he was going to kiss me and if I were to be honest with myself, I wanted it to happen, but I pulled away.

"I'm sorry... I ... I can't."

I was half expecting him to ask why, or assert himself and insist.

Instead, he just nodded and looked away from me. "I understand."

For some reason, that irritated me. *How could he understand when I myself didn't?* I realized then how much it irked me that he could see me as so soft and fragile. It made me feel weak, but it didn't change the fact that I wasn't ready for that kiss.

That night, just before I could escape to peaceful slumber, I realized why. It was because I was certain that if I ever gave in to him in that way, if I surrendered to that kiss, I wouldn't be able to keep myself from falling for him. If I ever allowed myself to fall in love with Derek Novak, I was certain that I would forever be a captive of The Shade.

CHAPTER 22: DEREK

That moment in the Sun Room haunted me as I watched her sleep beside me. She backed away when I tried to kiss her. Had it been any other woman, I wouldn't have hesitated to force my way and get that kiss anyway. But it was Sofia. She wasn't just any woman.

I wanted her to want me, but after all she'd seen, after everything she'd been through, I couldn't blame her for shying away from me. I understood, but it didn't change how painful it felt.

She shifted on the bed, her blanket getting tossed to her side, showing a generous amount of skin on her soft legs. I swallowed hard. Nights with Sofia were torturous. To have her there, beautiful and so damn close to me, always reminded me of how much I wanted her. Her nightwear would almost always get displaced and show her neck and shoulders, practically begging me to take a bite.

I rose from the bed, unsure of myself and what I was feeling for her. It made me sick to think about the danger she was facing.

Gwen's murderer still hadn't been found, though in my gut, I knew who it was. I just couldn't bear to admit it. The familiar sick feeling settled inside my stomach as I walked toward the large windows leading to the balcony that overlooked the Pavilion's magnificent view. The night was black, with no trace of the moon's rays anywhere.

I felt as dark as that night.

I remembered seeing Lucas earlier that day whispering something in Sofia's ear. I noticed how her entire body tensed and how she was obviously attempting to hold back her anger. I didn't do anything about it. I pretended I didn't see anything.

When Sofia approached me, she acted the same way I did. Like nothing just happened. She smiled and held my hand. She told me she had a surprise for me. Her warm auburn hair and her radiant smile reminded me of sunshine more than the Sun Room ever could.

"Derek?" Sofia purred from behind me. "Do you ever sleep?"

I shook my head as I turned around. "Not as much as you do." I caught my breath at how stunning she looked, her deep green eyes gazing up at me. I felt like a boy talking to a girl for the first time. Sofia always managed to make me feel quite unhinged.

As I approached her, a pensive expression replaced the smile on her face. I sat over the edge of the bed and rubbed a hand over her hip.

"Is something wrong?"

She placed her hand over mine, brushing her fingers over my skin. The motion sent chills running through my body. Our eyes met and for a moment, nothing else mattered other than to have her there with me. I realized at that moment that I couldn't even think of a life without her. I felt selfish and guilty for keeping her there, even when her life was in danger, but I reasoned to myself that there was no other way.

"What's on your mind, Derek?" she whispered.

"You…" I saw no reason to lie "… I can't imagine life without you."

She sat up on the bed and reached to touch my cheek. There was no tension, no apprehension between either of us anymore. We remained guarded when around others, but once alone, there was a familiarity, a rhythm, almost a dance between us. It was one of the reasons she made me feel so … known.

"I don't know if this means anything to you," she began to say, and then hesitated as if she were planning her next words carefully.

I inwardly scoffed at her statement. It was rare for any word coming from those sweet lips of hers not to mean something to me.

"What?" I coaxed her.

I doubted she could've possibly known how moved I was by what she said next.

"From the moment I got here, all I've wanted to do is escape and go back home, but Derek…" she leant toward me and placed a gentle kiss over my cheek "…you've begun to feel like home."

****

Home.

The word was still circling in my mind the next morning.

I sat on the living room couch, my eyes glued to one of the members of the Elite – Claudia, a capricious and vain female vampire who managed to convince my father and brother that she had our family's best interests at heart.

I still wasn't sure about her true motives. Before my sleep, she had made more than one attempt to foster a relationship with me. I found her very presence, beautiful as she was, repugnant. Still, she requested my audience and I had no reason to deny her that request.

But I could barely hear what she was saying – meaningless pleasantries that meant nothing to me, because my mind was still so wrapped up in what Sofia had implied last night.

Did she mean that I am the reason she would want to remain here at The Shade?

Claudia finished her babbling and waited for some sort of response. A social cue. I eyed her from head to foot and discarded everything she'd just been jabbering about.

"I see you've done quite well for yourself, Claudia," I commented, noting her outfit and the aura of extravagance surrounding her.

"It's all thanks to you, isn't it, my *prince*?" she smiled.

"Let's not lose ourselves in small talk. Why did you want to see me?" I said, eager to get to business and get rid of her.

I momentarily eyed the young man standing behind her by the door, waiting on her. Blonde, well-built – very much the type Claudia enjoyed exploiting. I remembered why I detested being around this vampire who was at least thirty years older than me, though she was turned at the tender age of seventeen.

Claudia's long lashes fluttered as she straightened in her seat. "Other than to pay my beloved prince homage, of course, I'm just really curious."

"Curious about what?"

"Curious about *whom*, you mean. Well, I've been hearing so much about your beautiful, redheaded pet. I was curious to find out what kind of girl was able to get Derek Novak himself all tied up in a knot."

I grimaced. Claudia's interest in Sofia was something I needed to dispel at all costs. Before I could even open my mouth to answer, however, I heard Sofia's laughter coming from outside. She and the girls had gone out for a walk, escorted by Sam and Kyle.

It was now too late. Sofia skipped through the front door with a smile on her face, her green eyes twinkling with delight.

Claudia instantly stood up, turned and eyed Sofia from head to toe.

"So, this is *her*." She said, enviously.

As if that weren't already bad enough, something else about the awkward situation began eating at me. Apart from the obvious disdain for Sofia that Claudia held in her eyes, I was agitated by the look of pure shock on Sofia's face the moment she laid eyes on Claudia's slave.

"Ben," she gasped, tears suddenly moistening her eyes.

The same amount of shock was evident in the boy's face upon seeing her. His face paled as fearful concern replaced his sallow and indifferent expression. Sofia rushed forward and threw her arms around him - and he returned her embrace with just as much passion. As he leaned his chin over the top of her head, he looked my way. I could almost hear the accusations and the threats he was hurling at me. It was obvious that he feared for Sofia, that he was worrying about what I could've already done to her.

A snide smirk formed on Claudia's face as she stared at the reunion between her slave and mine.

"Interesting. Very interesting indeed."

I stood there, not knowing what to do. Or what to think. But I was sure that what I was seeing right there in front of me, was Sofia embracing her reason to leave The Shade forever.

CHAPTER 23: SOFIA

Chills ran down my spine as I eased into Ben's strong arms which wrapped tightly around me. There were so many questions going through my mind. I didn't know whether to be happy or horrified that I would see him in a place like The Shade.

"With all due respect, my beloved prince," Derek's guest purred seductively, "I don't like other girls touching what's mine, and from the look on your face, I don't think you're enjoying this sight either."

I could feel Ben's whole body tense the moment she spoke. It was sickening to think of the possibilities surrounding his presence at The Shade. I wanted to speak, to say something to him, ask him at least one of the questions swimming around in my head, but I knew that the moment I tried, I wouldn't be able to hold back the sobs. I wanted to hold on to him, but we both knew that we had to let go. Holding on was nothing but trouble … for both of us, so we reluctantly distanced ourselves and stood still in front of the man and woman keeping us captive.

"Who is he, Sofia?" Derek asked.

I didn't miss the tension in his voice.

"A friend."

His blonde guest wrinkled her nose.

"*Just* a friend?!"

"The best I ever had," I replied, my voice breaking in the process as tears spilled down my cheeks.

"Grant me a request, will you, Claudia?" Derek spoke up, his eyes fixed on me.

I couldn't make out the expression on his face. I wasn't sure if my affection for Ben had annoyed him. For some reason, my heart went out to him. I felt like I wanted to assure him that Ben being there changed nothing between us, but that was a lie.

It changed *everything.* I remembered what I told him the night before – that he'd begun to feel like home. I could never forget the way he looked at me afterwards – like I meant the world to him. I was so moved by how this strong and powerful man could look at me that way. It was strange, because at that moment, I felt like I had the power and he was the one who was vulnerable and at *my* mercy.

As I stood beside Ben, fearing for him, I took another look at the master I'd grown to deeply care for, and began to wonder.

Is it possible for me to break Derek Novak?

I snapped out of my internal monologue when I realized how disgustedly Claudia was looking at me.

"Yes, *your Majesty*? What can I do for you?"

Derek made his way to her, his hand snaking along her waist from behind as he pulled her back against his body. She didn't hide the delight in her face as she eyed me as if she'd somehow won something over me. My gut clenched. I had the strangest reaction to seeing Derek touch another woman the way he was touching her. It was quite similar to the way I felt when I saw Ben on the beach with Tanya, but this was different … more intense … more painful. I hated to admit it, but I was jealous. I wanted to give in to the irrational urge to slap Derek across the face and rip Claudia's hair out, but since that was not an option, I looked away instead.

What Derek said next completely crushed all my resolve to ignore him for the rest of the day.

"As you already know, Claudia, the lovely Sofia has become very precious to me, and she seems to have quite a liking for your slave here. You've come to pay me homage, have you not?"

Claudia's face tensed. "I have."

"It will please me greatly if you give me the boy. My slave, Gwen, was murdered as you may have heard … I need a new one."

"Surely there are others…" Claudia tried to protest. "I know you well enough to know that you don't have a thing for young men the way *others* do."

Derek's grip tightened on her waist, his mouth speaking directly to her ear. "As I said, Sofia has obviously taken a liking to him. I don't want anyone else, because it's this one Sofia wants. What pleases her pleases me. Do you dare deny me this request, *Claudia?*"

Claudia pulled away from him and straightened to her full height, as if trying to regain an air of dignity I doubted she had to begin with. We all knew that to deny Derek his request would be fatal on her part. He was her prince, and he was asking for but one slave. There was no reason for her to refuse. She frowned and shot me a glare before eyeing Ben with unbridled lust.

"I rather liked this one, but I have more than I know what to do with." She approached Ben and caressed his cheek with the back of her hand. Her eyes didn't leave mine as she stood on her tiptoes to kiss Ben's lips.

I looked at Ben and it was clear that he felt toward her the same way I felt toward Lucas. The sick feeling that settled in my stomach wouldn't go away. I refused to even start imagining what Ben had endured while at The Shade.

Claudia took one last look at Derek.

"I could never deny you any*thing*, dear prince. I shall visit again soon." She scowled and walked away.

With her gone, I grabbed Ben's hand and pulled him against my body again. I eyed Derek and mouthed a sincere *thank you* his way. He nodded and forced a smile. Having Ben there, I found myself confused, because while I was ecstatic to see my best friend, what I felt most at that moment was how much I adored Derek for what he did. I held on tightly to Ben almost in hopes of regaining my attraction to him if I held on tight enough.

"I hate her," Ben hissed in my ear. "I hate them all."

I hugged him tighter.

"Don't worry, Ben. You're okay now. Derek will keep us both safe."

"Don't be a fool, Sofia. We need to get out of this place before he decides that he's tired of you and kills us both."

The idea made me sick to my stomach. *What will happen if Derek ever realizes that I'm no one special... and decides he's had enough of me?* I wanted to believe that such a thing couldn't ever happen, but Ben always had a way of swaying me with his words. I gave Derek a worried glance. It felt as though I'd just lost him.

CHAPTER 24: DEREK

I hated the tension. Since she moved into my bedroom, Sofia and I naturally developed a familiarity. It was like we just knew how to adjust to each other. Of course, there were times when I was greatly tempted to take a sip of her blood, but it wasn't anything a glass of blood from Vivienne couldn't fix.

The night Ben arrived, however, it was like we'd become strangers again. The large room suddenly felt too small for the two of us. Any form of balance we'd developed over time completely disappeared. She was slipping away from my fingers by the minute.

Finally, she was lying down on her side of the bed while I sat over the edge of mine, fully intending to lose myself in a book. She was the one who eventually broke the silence.

"Thank you, Derek. For what you did."

I had no desire to talk about the boy, so I ignored her thankfulness and changed the topic.

"Lucas approached you earlier. What did he tell you?"

"Nothing," she responded a little too quickly. "You know your brother ... says a lot of meaningless things."

"From the way you reacted, what he said looked far from meaningless." I remembered what Corrine told me about Sofia's psychological condition and how it was impossible for her not to remember what happened the night she was attacked.

"Has he been hurting you, Sofia?"

She didn't respond. "It doesn't matter."

"What do you mean it doesn't matter?" I gripped the sheets of the bed, wondering why I was asking questions whose answers I wouldn't even know how to act on. "Has he?"

Sofia sat up on the bed and held my wrist.

"Why are you acting like this? You've seen Lucas and I interact countless times."

"Interact? Is that what you do with Lucas?"

I knew I was being irrational and unreasonable, but the image of Sofia with Ben embracing was burning away all logical thought and reason in my mind.

"Has something been going on between you and my brother, Sofia?"

"Me and Lucas?!" She looked angry as she spoke through gritted teeth, like it was the most disgusting thing she'd ever heard of. "That's madness, Derek. I would *never...*"

I moved fast, pushing her down against the bed. I quickly grabbed her wrists and pinned them with one hand over her head and knelt on the bed, straddling her hips.

Her eyes grew wide in question.

"What are you doing?" she asked in a small, broken voice. "Wait! *Don't...*"

I grabbed her jaw non-too-gently. It was the first time I had treated her in an untoward fashion since the first time we met. I felt like I was losing her and that it was beyond my control. I wanted to regain some form of control and unreasonable as it was, I was taking my agitation out on her.

"You're *mine*, Sofia. Many things have changed between us, but *that* hasn't changed."

She didn't respond. Instead, she just looked at me in a way she hadn't in a long time. She looked at me with fear.

That woke me up from my momentary burst of insanity. I let go of her and got off her, feeling like the biggest fool to ever walk the earth. I couldn't look at her. I couldn't even bear being in the same room with her. I didn't deserve her.

I knew I was lying when I reminded her that the fact that she was mine hadn't changed. No matter what alpha male act I might pull off in trying to intimidate her, I knew the truth. She was no longer mine. At some point during all those nights I'd spent with her, I'd become *hers*.

CHAPTER 25: SOFIA

No words could explain how shaken I was. It was so unlike Derek and I couldn't understand how he could do something like that, or why he would do it. Doubts assailed my mind.

Was Ben right? Was this Derek getting tired of me?

I remained motionless on the bed long after he stormed out of the room off to … I didn't want to know where. I was trembling, unsure of what to make of what just happened. All sense of security I felt whenever I was in that bedroom began to wash away and I found myself terrified.

Yet, after a bout of self-introspection, I realized that though I resented him for treating me the way he did, I felt worried for Derek. It wasn't like him to act the way he did … something was wrong. I looked back on the reason for his outburst. *He thinks there's something going on between me and Lucas.* I wanted to explain to him how that couldn't be further from the truth, but how was I to do that?

Wanting to draw my mind away from what happened, I climbed out of bed and pulled on a silk robe over my nightwear. Still plagued by worrisome thoughts, I retreated to the room that contained memories of Derek's smile, of a dance with music that only played in Derek's head, of a kiss that I'd wanted so much, but couldn't allow to happen.

I opened the door to the Sun Room and was surprised to find Ben standing there with a look of pure bliss and unveiled fascination on his face. After Derek "acquired" Ben, we spent the rest of the day together – up until the point when I had to go to Derek's room to get some sleep. Ben actually suggested that I stay with him, but much to his dismay, I declined. I knew that should Lucas attack that night, I would only put Ben in danger if I was found with him.

The time spent with Ben felt awkward and forced. The Shade had changed him in ways I knew I wouldn't be able to fully understand. Not many words were spoken between us. We just satisfied ourselves with being around the other. I knew he had his own questions for me, and I had mine, but both of us were afraid to hear the answers. I wouldn't know how to handle it if Ben started telling me something awful about his experience at The Shade. I didn't even know if I could handle telling him about what Lucas had been putting me through and why I couldn't possibly tell Derek.

So that relaxed and almost joyous expression on his face as he viewed the Sun Room was a precious sight to behold.

"We call it the Sun Room," I said, surprising him. "I designed the room myself. You like it?"

I stepped inside, putting a smile on my face and trying to forget Derek. I couldn't deny the sense of pride I had upon seeing Ben's face and how enamored he seemed by the illusion of the sun streaming through the room.

But it reminded me so much of the reaction on Derek's face when I first brought him to the room, that it almost felt like I was cheating on Derek just by being there with Ben.

"You did this?" Ben asked. "Sofia, this is … incredible."

He sighed as he approached the mural of the beach on the wall.

"What I wouldn't give to see the sun … This place and its darkness…" He shuddered. "This room is a refuge. What made you think of this?"

I bit my lip as I stared at him.

"Derek told me that he hadn't seen sunlight in five hundred years. I could swear he missed it, so that's where I got the idea, and…"

Ben withdrew his hand from the mural he was touching and admiring. It was as if the mention of Derek being involved in the creative process suddenly made the mural unappealing.

"So you did this for *him*?" He asked incredulously.

"Well, yeah…" I admitted. "That - and I also missed the sun." I didn't like where the conversation was going.

"How could you do anything for him? For any of their kind?" His tone was accusing and intense. "You're his *slave*, Sofia. How could you live with that?"

I didn't have the answers to the questions he was throwing my way. What could I possibly say to him? That Derek was different? That he wasn't like the others? All I knew was that over the time I'd been there, Derek had begun to mean a lot to me. Even after what he did earlier, and no matter how hurt and confused I was by it, I still had trouble seeing Derek in a negative light. How could I even begin to explain this to Ben? I wrapped my arms around Ben's waist from behind, hoping to take his thoughts away from the vampires.

"Let's just forget about *them* for now, can we please? I missed you so much."

"I can't just *forget*, Sofia," Ben spat. "You have no idea what that bitch put me through."

There was an edge to his voice. Jaded. Broken. Cynical. There was no sorrow left. Just pure hatred. Completely unlike the happy-go-lucky Ben I used to know. He turned around to face me, his eyes blazing with bitterness and spite.

"I never would've thought that it would be you – the girl Claudia's been harping on about, the human who stole the vampire prince's heart. You couldn't possibly understand how much it crushes me to see that you were taken captive too, that their kind can ruin you any way they please. And after everything, it almost seems like you've fallen in love with *him*."

I swallowed hard. *Fallen in love? With Derek?* I couldn't lie to myself. I knew I was in danger of falling for him, but whether that had happened already … whether I'd actually fallen for him, I still wasn't sure of. I felt as if I didn't need to defend whatever it was I had with Derek to Ben, nor did I want to, so I focused on Ben instead. I knew that there was no escaping where this conversation was going. I geared myself up for the worst.

"What happened to you, Ben? How did you get here? What has she been doing to you?"

There was a long pause before Ben heaved a sigh and began to explain. "You didn't return to the villa the night of your birthday. I was worried sick. I waited for hours but you didn't show up, so I started looking for you. That's when she found me. She took me to her penthouse and I've been there since. This was the first time she allowed me out after I tried to escape."

"You … you tried to escape? What happened?"

He smiled bitterly. "See for yourself."

He pulled off his white woolen shirt.

I gasped at the sight, tears spilling from my eyes, as I clamped a palm over my mouth. His upper torso was covered in scars, cut after cut marred his body. I trembled as I ran a finger over one of them.

"How were you able to *survive* this, Ben?"

"That's the last round of torture you see there. She used a dagger to cut me, deep enough to scar, but shallow enough not to cause internal damage. The first two rounds of torture, she beat me up to a bloody pulp and then made me drink her blood so I could heal, so she could torture me again."

It took everything I had to keep myself from vomiting.

"These creatures are evil savages, Sofia. All of them. They don't have a conscience just as much as they don't have a life. You might think this prince of theirs has a heart in him somewhere, but he doesn't, Sofia. No matter how he's taken care of you, he's still a vampire. And whenever he lays his eyes on you, all he sees is a beautiful young woman he can sink his teeth into."

And yet … he hasn't. No matter how tempted he was, he never gave in. I looked up at my best friend, wanting to agree with him, but still finding my inner conscience standing in defense of Derek. It made me feel guilty, because after all Ben had been through, he deserved to have me on his side, but all I could think of was the smile on Derek's face and the way he looked at me when he motioned to kiss me. No matter how much I tried to recall the negative behavior of my captor, I found that I didn't have it in me to see Derek as a savage … simply because he wasn't one.

"I can't blame you for thinking that. Claudia certainly is," was the compromise I could come up with to appease Ben.

"But you think your prince isn't?"

"Derek has his flaws, but he's far from being a savage."

Ben responded by cupping my face with his large hands and

planting a kiss over my forehead.

"You're so wrong, Sofia, and for your sake, I hope we can find a way out of here before his true colors come out."

"Well, well, well … what do we have here?"

As if the thoughts Ben was laying on me weren't enough of a burden to bear, I now had to hear the terrifying sound of Lucas' voice.

"You're one naughty girl, Sofia. I hate it enough when I see Derek touch you, but now *this*?"

Before I could even start formulating a response, Lucas had both Ben and I backed up against a wall, his powerful hands keeping us both in place by our necks. Lucas' glare settled on Ben.

"If it isn't Claudia's slave… Weren't you the one serving us during those pleasurable rendezvous I spent with your mistress?"

Ben struggled against Lucas' grasp. However, he was weaponless and we both knew there wasn't much he could do to harm Lucas.

"Welcome to the Pavilion, boy," Lucas grinned, showing amusement over Ben's failure to get away from him. "First lesson you ought to learn is that you *never* touch what's mine."

Ben spat on his face and snarled, "Sofia is neither yours nor your brother's! She belongs with me."

Infuriated by Ben's insolence, Lucas growled and hurled Ben to the other side of the room. Ben's head hit the wall and he fell to the ground unconscious. I let out a scream and tried to rush toward Ben, but Lucas' cold grip held me back. His manic glare focused on me.

"I think it's time I got what I want from you. It's been long enough. Don't you agree, my little twig?"

Chapter 26: Derek

What have I done? After the way I behaved, I might as well have just delivered her to that boy on a silver platter.

From the moment I left Sofia trembling in my bed, I'd done nothing but chastise myself for my behavior. I couldn't believe myself. I actually accused her of being with Lucas, whom I was certain had been tormenting her over the past weeks – all out of my jealousy over this *friend* of hers. I walked through the woods hoping to clear my mind, but not succeeding at all. If anything, I was more confused than ever. My walk and the time I spent thinking only made me paranoid as my mind started to wonder what scene I might walk into upon my return. I was gearing myself up to stop myself from ripping someone's head off in case I found Sofia in bed with this *friend* of hers.

Get a grip, Derek, I kept telling myself. I was being irrational. Sofia said the boy was her best friend. *Believe her.*

Then I remembered how she looked at him ... how I was certain she'd never looked at me that way before and my paranoia once again kicked in.

There's no way that boy is 'just a friend'.

I only returned to the Pavilion after I felt I was ready for the worst possible scenario upon reaching the penthouse, but nothing could've prepared me for what I found.

The first thing I noticed was Sam and Kyle waking up from unconsciousness on the living room floor.

"What happened?!" I shouted, panicking.

"Sun ... Room," was all Sam managed to say. "Ben's ... there ... too."

My gut clenched. I felt betrayed that Sofia would be with any other person in the Sun Room who wasn't me. I forced my jealousy aside, knowing that something was terribly wrong and that I had to get my head on straight.

When I reached the room, I froze in shock at the sight of Ben's unconscious form on the ground and Sofia whimpering as she tried in vain to push my brother away from her.

Lucas had her up a wall, naked from the waist up. His teeth sank into her neck as his hands freely groped her body. He was quivering as he enjoyed the sensations the feel of her skin provided and greedily drank her blood.

I lost all sense of control and attacked my brother, making a huge crack in the wall as I smashed him into it.

Lucas actually had the gall to laugh. I punched his face with such great force, I half-expected his neck to crack from the way his head swung violently to the side.

I was sure that he had gone completely mad based on the wild expression on his face. But I was wrong. He knew exactly what he was doing.

"I can't let you have her, brother," he spat at me – a mixture of her blood and his own. "I will lose everything the moment she becomes completely yours."

I didn't understand what he was saying. I didn't want to. I just wanted to end him, end this bitter rivalry we'd had for so many years. I was far more powerful than him and his struggles to get away from me didn't do him any good. I retrieved the wooden stake I kept on my person all the time.

"Is that *the* wooden stake? The same one you used all those years as a hunter?"

Lucas showed no fear. He knew me well enough to realize how important family was to me, but he grossly underestimated how valuable Sofia had become. After all that time I spent weighing who mattered more to me – my brother or Sofia, at that moment, the choice was crystal clear: I had every intention of stabbing that stake through his heart to protect the woman I loved.

I caught my own thoughts. I tensed at the realization. *The woman I loved. That's how I saw Sofia.* Now that Lucas had tasted her blood, he would become even more of a threat to her.

I raised the stake and aimed it at my brother's heart.

The smirk on his face disappeared when he realized I had every intention of killing him. He had gone too far. He cowered in fear when I made the motion to stab him. Relief washed over his face when someone stood to his defense.

"Derek, no…" Sofia's soft voice called to me.

"You're not safe with him," I said through gritted teeth.

"I never was." She panted.

I could tell from the way she spoke that she was conflicted, most likely debating against her own reasons for keeping me from driving that stake into Lucas' heart.

"Then why should he live?! He has to die!"

Sofia's answer reminded me why I adored her so much.

"If you kill your own brother, Derek, you might never be able to forgive me. Or worse than that, you might never be able to forgive yourself."

She knew me – all sides of me – but she never treated me like a creature of the dark. When she looked at me, it felt as if she still saw someone capable of light.

I dropped the stake and loosened my hold on my brother. He lost no time in taking advantage of what he most likely perceived as a momentary lapse of sanity, and rushed out of the room. *He hasn't changed at all.* Lucas was a coward and a bully. He never did stand up to those who were more powerful than him, but he found enjoyment in preying on the weak.

That was why I was certain that as long as she was at The Shade, Sofia would never be safe.

Lucas would stalk her and hunt her like he would an animal. He wouldn't relent until he'd had his fill of her. Unless I killed him.

I flinched when I felt her soft hand brush against my arm. I turned around and forced myself to look at her. She tossed the pieces left of her nightgown over herself, trying to cover herself up. I ripped off my shirt immediately and pulled it over her head. I once again made a cut on my palm and made her drink my blood. It was at that moment that I realized her friend was already awake, watching us – specifically *me* – with untrusting eyes.

I ignored him, and waited for Sofia's wounds to heal, my eyes fixed particularly on Lucas' bite marks on her neck.

"I'm so sorry, Sofia. I failed you again."

She looked so pale and weak from the attack, as she shook her head. "No, Derek. You *saved* me… again."

"Sofia … did he rape you?" I couldn't look into her eyes. The question obviously broke her heart and I hated that I had to ask it. She shook her head.

"No. He didn't," she assured me.

However, I could tell that he had done everything but. It sickened me that I could be related to such a monster.

"You have to go, Sofia."

At first, there was shock in her eyes, and then confusion.

"What do you mean?"

"I'll let you leave The Shade."

I'll let you leave me was actually what I wanted to say. I wanted her to tell me that she'd rather stay, that she trusted me enough to protect her. She didn't. It crushed me when she embraced me instead and said, "*Thank you.*"

Chapter 27: Sofia

I wanted to take the girls with me and insisted on it. Derek wouldn't hear of it. In fact, he simply ignored me. He wouldn't even look at me. But he looked at Ben and said, "Protect her."

Ben just looked at him incredulously as if to say that he didn't need to be *told* to do that. Ben hated Derek and saw no reason to be grateful for what he was doing.

I saw differently. I knew how much Derek was risking by helping us escape. He was severely compromising the safety of everyone at The Shade by letting us go. He was giving his kind a reason to question his rule. I feared for him — so much that I found myself debating if I even wanted to leave.

What he told Ben next tore me apart.

"Make sure she gets home safe."

Home.

I told him that he'd begun to feel like home, and at that moment,

I knew I was deceiving myself if I was trying to convince myself that by leaving The Shade, I'd be going back home. At that point, I wasn't sure where home was anymore, but it didn't change the fact that both my and Ben's lives were in severe danger by staying there. Mine because of Lucas' determination to have me. Ben's because of his connection to me … and Claudia.

So, the escape went on as planned.

Derek knew The Shade well. He knew where to go and what to do in order to remain hidden. Considering that Corrine had already told him about my LLI, that too was a risk. He knew that I would remember every single detail of my escape. It meant that should I ever return to The Shade, I would be well acquainted with the road to freedom, even in the dark. With every step I took nearer to the port where Derek had already secured a ride for us to return to the beach from where we were first stolen, I realized how much I didn't want to go. Not because I'd suddenly found a special spot in my heart for The Shade, but because I didn't want to be anywhere he wasn't.

I hated that he wouldn't even look at me. When the port came into sight, I'd had enough. Ben was holding my hand and Derek was trailing behind us, making sure no one was following. I stopped walking, hoping that Derek would bump into me. He didn't. As always, he was aware of my every move.

Ben pulled on my hand. His face fell when I wriggled my hand away from his grasp.

"I need to talk to Derek," was all the explanation I gave him.

Ben didn't look happy, but he nodded, glaring at Derek before moving forward – a safe distance away from us.

I turned around to face Derek. I wanted him to look at me. But he looked away.

"Don't be this way, Derek."

"What way?"

"Distant."

"Why not? That's what you'll be once you leave The Shade."

It was the first time I fully realized that once I left, it was goodbye forever. It wasn't like I could just go online and video chat with him.

"That's exactly why I can't bear this, Derek." I held back a sob. "We've been through too much … I'd like to think that we've grown to mean a lot to each other."

This was a painful understatement. And I hated how I sounded so formal. At that moment, it felt like he meant *everything* to me and with all my heart, I wished that he felt the same. I tried hard to hold back the tears as I continued my attempt to speak out loud what was eating me away inside.

"To part this way … barely even talking, barely even looking at each other … I don't know how to handle it. I can't bear it."

I choked before I could say the words that I knew would forever haunt me.

I love you too much to leave everything hanging like this.

My spine tingled when he reached for me, his fingers caressing my cheek and brushing through my hair. Before I could even make sense of what was happening, his lips pressed against mine – hungry, passionate, demanding. His tongue pushed between my lips – claiming, exploring, tasting. I found myself tensing against his touch, and then easing into it. I wanted it. I was just as hungry as he was, just as passionate. It shook me to realize how much I wanted this, how much I wanted him. Every second that kiss lasted was another second for the truth to sink in.

I've already stopped even thinking about a life that doesn't have Derek Novak in it.

When our lips parted, I found myself gasping for breath, but desperate for more. He held me tight. I sensed his need, his desire for me to stay, when he whispered into my ear:

"You don't want to leave."

At that, I broke down into tears. He was right. Whether I liked it or not, home had become wherever Derek Novak was.

Epilogue: Vivienne

I was jolted from my sleep, knowing fully well what had just occurred the moment their lips touched. I grabbed the sheets of my bed as chills ran through my body. I saw glimpses of it in a vision. Derek and his beloved Sofia sharing that kiss … It was the kiss that set our destiny in stone. The game had just begun. My mind's eye began to fill with flood upon flood of conflicting premonitions of what was to come. All of it confusing. Every single one disturbing.

Neither Derek nor Sofia had any clue of what they had up against them. Truth be told, I didn't fully understand either.

I sensed the dread of what was to come forming deep within me. I sensed Lucas' resentment and my father's conflict over his love for Derek and his love for power. I sensed the growing strength of the hunters. But more than anything, I sensed the intensity of emotion Derek held for Sofia.

My brother had unknowingly chosen his mate. All that was left now was for her to prove herself worthy of such a place. I'd never felt more unsure of what the future held than I did at that moment. But there was one thing I knew for certain:

Blood would be shed.

Want to read the next part of Derek and Sofia's story?
A Shade Of Vampire 2: A Shade Of Blood is available now!

Visit www.bellaforrest.net for more information.

Note from the Author

Dear Shaddict,

If you want to stay informed about my latest book releases, visit this website to subscribe to my new releases email list: www.forrestbooks.com

Also, if you subscribe, you'll be automatically entered to win a signed copy of A Shade Of Vampire.

You can also check out my other novels by visiting my website: www.bellaforrest.net

And don't forget to come say hello on Facebook.
I'd love to meet you personally, and sometimes Derek Novak takes over as manager of the page:
www.facebook.com/AShadeOfVampire

Thank you for reading!

Love,
Bella

Printed in Great Britain
by Amazon.co.uk, Ltd.,
Marston Gate.